IN T
ABSENCE
OF LIGHT

By,
B. E. Brown

Devin,
You are the best
Story - make it a good
one :) Love,
B.E. Brown

Prologue

DESPERATION

Wednesday July 16th

Harold Pinchly glanced in his rear view mirror. Nothing. The road was empty. This knowledge did not stop the beads of sweat that rolled down his face. He glanced at his refection in the rear view mirror and wondered at the old man that looked back at him. It wasn't a face that he recognized, balding, salt and pepper beard and heavy eyes. No, the man looking back at him was not who he remembered being, but it was who he was.

Harold drove along the lone highway, white knuckles on the steering wheel, passing small towns with names he couldn't remember as he crossed over the border of Wyoming and Montana, speeding through an area of the country that wasn't found on most maps. He had thought the remoteness of the area a safe haven at one time, yet now the isolation seemed to smother him.

Harold touched the breast pocket of his shirt. Good, the flash drive was still there, along with a small scrap of paper, Landry Alston, 1453 Greenwald Ave, Denver, Colorado, written across it in heavy hand printed letters.

This was his goal, his only hope. Harold Pinchly knew that he had one shot, one chance or all his research, and all his hopes for salvation, would be gone. He had to get to the Billings, Montana airport; he had to get to Landry Alston. He had spent too much time hiding out, too much time figuring out his next step. He knew he had to act.

But, there was something else, something deeper that Harold also knew. It was a truth so strong, so irrevocable that it was etched into his very bones. Harold Pinchly knew that he was going to die.

2

1

DYING OF THE LIGHT

"Hello?" Emily's voice echoed off the black glittering walls of the cavern. There was no answer. She cleared her throat and tried again, this time it came out a half panicked yell. "Hello!" Still the only sound that she heard was the frantic beating of her own heart.

Little over an hour earlier, she, along with the rest of her "Spelunking 101" class, had followed Professor Stevens into the caves. The path had twisted and turned but the ceiling had been high enough to walk upright in. The students studied the rock formations, the different types of sediment, sketched in their notebooks the layers of rock and tried out their new gear.

Emily's spelunking equipment had been furnished by the local undergraduate college and included her helmet, helmet lamp, two extra hand held flash lights, water proof matches, a utility candle (used mostly for a source of warmth) and a handbook. She had purchased the hiking boots and climbing gloves on her own.

The class had met outside Professor Stevens's office early that morning and piled into two separate vans that would carry them up the Big Horn Mountains located in Wyoming. The general excitement, anticipation and restless chatter shared by the students, made the two hour forty-five minute drive from Northwest College in Powell to their destination at the mouth of the caves, fly by.

The mixture had been amazing. Some of the group had taken the class every semester and considered themselves to be "hard core cavers"; others just needed the P.E. credit to graduate the following year. Still others, like Emily's best friend, Bernadette, and herself, had taken the class for a much more superficial reason.

****

Emily sat back on her legs and stared down the darkened tunnel. She had only turned around for a moment, just a few seconds, to pull herself free of a sharp rock that had caught her pant leg. She had been scooting on her hands and knees in the confined space behind the group. The class had voted and taken one of two ways out. This route was shorter, but wasn't high enough for even the shortest in the class to walk upright. Emily could still hear talking and see lights when she noticed her boot was untied. This had been her mistake. By the time she turned around all traces of the group had vanished.

****

The afternoon sun was bright and warm on Bernadette's face as she emerged from the cramped tunnel. A hand was placed in front of her offering assistance to her feet. She took it, grateful to stand upright again and stretch her legs. Crawling out through the smaller maze of tunnels had been voted on by the group before they headed out of the main cavern. She had not been particularly excited to spend the next thirty minutes on her hands and knees, but had been outvoted in the process.

Most of the students were already out of the cramped space and milling around, enjoying the bright warmth of the afternoon sun. Off to the right Professor Stevens was taking a head count. A very pretty blonde girl, Bernadette could never remember her name, was trying to talk to the Professor as he did so. The older gentleman nodded from time to time and smiled in her direction. It was obvious that he was trying to keep his mind on the task and his attractive student was giving him as much trouble as possible.

Bernadette pulled off her gloves and stuffed them into her pocket, then pulled off her helmet and let her hair blow in the breeze. She walked out of the cover of the trees so that she could more fully drink in the afternoon sun. It was early May in Wyoming and the sun was bright and warm, not as warm as the native Las Vegas twenty-two year old was used to, but after being cramped into a dark and cold cave, any sun at all was welcome.

As she stood, rooted for the moment to the spot, she noticed the other members of the class milling around, some heading toward the vans to gather their lunches and some padding down a nearby trail to the restrooms. Before moving to Wyoming as a teenager Bernadette had never even seen an outhouse let alone used one. It still made her thankful for the modern day convenience of a flushing toilet.

****

Emily wished they had not taken this route out of the cavern. It was no more than three feet tall and she ached to stand up. She had to reassure herself that as soon as the rest of the group had vacated, Professor Stevens would notice that someone was missing and come looking for her.

His short lecture before entering the cave had consisted of a safety lesson. She could still hear his words in her head. "Buddy system, if you get separated from the group stay put, and never leave your pack." This last piece of advice Emily had not listened so closely to. Each member had a small pack that carried their extra sources of light, a water bottle and a few energy bars.

Just before leaving the large cavern, Emily and Bernadette had changed buddies with two of the class's young men. Doug, the teacher's assistant, was to round out the

5

group and take the last position, but had been talked into going before Emily and her new companion, Tim.

Tim had then offered to carry Emily's pack on the way out. It was obvious that he was just trying to impress her and she had allowed herself to be taken in. As the group exited the large cavern on their way out Emily had been just behind Doug and Tim at the rear. Then as Tim came too close for comfort more than once and Emily had insisted that he go first, using claustrophobia as an easy out.

Emily was not by any means claustrophobic, but it had worked and she no longer felt her personal space being violated. Yet now she was alone and would have given anything to have kept her place in line. Placing her head in her hands she sat back against the cold rock, wishing that so many little things had gone differently.

Glancing at her wristwatch her heart sank. It was 12:30 and the group would have been out of the caves by now. She pleaded with the surrounding darkness to open up and reveal the welcome light of another's headlamp, but the pathways around her remained dark.

****

Bernadette was becoming frantic as panic gripped her heart. She had been positive that Emily had been just a few people behind her, now she wished they had never switched partners. She glanced around the gathering group again and counted.

"Bernadette, come sit with us." A friend waved to her from a nearby log. The small group of girls had been chatting and laughing while eating their sandwiches. She bit down on her lower lip as she walked slowly over to them.

"Have any of you seen Emily? I can't seem to find her." The girls looked at one another.

6

"She might be at the vans. I just saw Tim down there getting his lunch; she might still be with him," responded one of the girls.

"Or down at the bathrooms, I know a lot of people have been going back and forth," said another. The girls suggested all kinds of explanations as to why Bernadette had not seen her friend.

"She's got to be around someplace, I saw her pack lying over by the picnic table when I was talking to Professor Stevens." This coming from the pretty blonde that Bernadette had noticed talking to the Professor when she exited the cave.

"Thanks," Bernadette muttered, and took off in the direction of the picnic table. She rounded one of the larger trees as it came into view. Many of the "die hard" students sat around the table with Professor Stevens. As she neared, one of the heads turned in her direction. It was Doug, the teacher's assistant. He smiled at her as she came closer and Bernadette almost lost her footing.

"Careful." He had instinctively reached out an arm to steady her.

"Thank You." Feeling herself ready to blush as red as a tomato she gathered herself together and turned away. Douglas Arthur had been the sole reason that Emily and Bernadette had taken this class in the first place. At the end of their last semester the roommates had reviewed their schedules and found they both lacked P.E. credits.

The school offered a wide selection of outdoor activities but neither had been too keen on that idea and had instead opted for something a little more simplistic; Bowling 101. As they sat in the office waiting their turn, the tall, and extremely handsome, Douglas Arthur, had stopped in to drop off his own revised schedule. Striking up a conversation with the two girls, he had convinced them the only thing to do was take Spelunking 101. It sealed the deal for them when he just happened to mention that he would be the assistant for the class.

Emily had lost interest in Doug when she had seen the other members of the class. Bernadette, on the other hand, had, in fact found herself feeling quite the *opposite*. Bernadette found Doug fascinating and brilliant. He was well read, computer savvy, and on top of that he seemed to be a genuinely nice guy. A novelty.

The class had been easy enough, nothing too demanding, and the time spent in actual caves had been limited by the amount of time Professor Stevens had taken up in class talking about his many accomplishments. This was the last of three cave explorations the class would take before their final written exam; it had also been the easiest. Little equipment was required and neither was any real knowledge of spelunking. For the most part it had been a walk in the park, only the last part had been at all trying. There had been a few tunnels leading off the main trail and crawling through them had not been nearly as fun as some might think it would be.

Bernadette had made every attempt to, as casually as possible; make her presence known to the older man. Doug had been polite and helpful, but no more. Getting him to notice her had been hard, and now, even harder, as she felt trapped under his gaze.

"Are you okay Bern?" He asked, calling her by her nickname. For a full minute she was unaware that he was even talking to her.

"Oh...um... sure. I was just looking for Emily. I can't find her anywhere."

"Is this her pack?" One of the other students asked as he lifted the pack into the air.

"Yes." Bernadette felt a rush of relief. That meant that her friend had to be out of the cave.

"Have you walked down to the restrooms?" Again it was Doug that drew her attention, feeling his blue eyes piercing her to the bone.

"Not yet, I was going to…" She trailed off as Doug, with his well over six-foot frame towered over her own five-foot four-inch frame, got to his feet.

"I'll walk down with you." He waved a hand toward the small trail and motioned for her to go first. Swallowing hard, she took off down the path.

****

It was a surprise how cold the caves were. Emily had worn extra thick woolen socks with her boots, yet even with the extra layer, her toes had begun to chill, along with her fingers, which were tucked away inside her gloves. Her face was beginning to feel numb from the cold.

She looked at her watch again: 1:30. The class would have been out of the caves for over an hour. How long had it taken for them to reach the main cavern? The trip down had been much faster because of the size of the tunnels leading to the massive underground room. Someone should have reached her by now, she was sure of it. The thought was sobering. What if they hadn't noticed that she was missing?

More than the cold, the image of the vans filling up and pulling away tore at her with icy fingers. She shuttered and turned to face the direction the group had taken. The pathway curved up ahead and was lost in blackness.

"Stay put." She told herself out loud. The sound of her own voice was reassuring. "Stay where they can find you." She shifted position on the hard ground and felt her stomach grumble. Her pack came to mind and she reached absentmindedly for it. Gone! Given to Tim. She cursed herself for being so foolish. She didn't even really like the boy. He was nice, but that was it. There was no attraction, and yet, against her better judgment she had flirted with him openly, relishing any attention.

For a spilt second Emily was sure she had fallen asleep. She closed her eyes for a moment and found more darkness. Then it happened again, the light on the far wall of the tunnel flickered just a little, like someone blinking. Emily jumped at the sight.

"Oh, you have got to me kidding me!"

****

Bernadette found herself walking next to Doug as the trail widened. He hummed a tune under his breath as he looked around the trees. Neither said a word as they neared the small brick building.

Bernadette tried to keep her mind on Emily but was too preoccupied with the fact that a few moments before, his hand had brushed her fingers as they walked, arms swinging. She has secretly hoped that the brief encounter had not been an accident, but when nothing else happened she pushed the thought out of her mind.

"I'll stay… here." His words broke into her thoughts. They stood outside the Women's Restroom door. Doug leaned on a nearby tree; arms folded across his chest, his sandy brown hair rustled in the breeze. She smiled to herself and knocked on the door with the back of her hand. No answer. Reaching for the handle she pulled ever so slightly and the door swung open. Empty.

"She's not here." Fear for her friend again took over any other feelings or thoughts she might have had while being alone with Doug. "She wasn't with the other girls, she wasn't with the rest of the class at the picnic table, and no one I've talked to has seen her." Bernadette met Doug's eyes. There was no mistaking the worry that etched itself in her face.

Rubbing his chin he turned and started back up the trail. "Emily was right behind me, with Tim." He said more to himself than to anyone else. Bernadette had to run to keep up with his long strides.

"Where are we going?" She asked between breaths. Doug slowed down so she could catch up with him.

"Tim was her caving partner right? He must have seen her. We know her pack made it out." Doug stopped talking and quickened his step again. Soon the vans and picnic table came into view. The group had cleaned up after their lunch and had most of the equipment packed into the vans.

"Professor Stevens, can I speak to you for a moment?" Bernadette noticed a glint of something in Doug's eye as he asked the question. His jaw was clenched tight as he stepped away from her. "Tim, would you mind coming this way?" He waved to the blonde farm boy and the three men walked a bit down the dirt road. Bernadette hated being left out of the conversation, but the look on Doug's face as he talked to the two men, kept her at bay.

She watched intently as they talked. Doug was the only one facing her and he was talking fast. He nodded a few times, his face turning red. Then Professor Stevens turned to Tim and took him by the shoulders. The young man walked slowly back to the vans. Doug and the Professor didn't return as quickly. She could tell even from this distance that they were having a heated argument. It ended as quickly as it had started and both men were headed back in her direction.

Bernadette noticed the look of pain on Professor Stevens's face. He rubbed the balding spot on the back of his head in thought.

"Everyone, please gather round." He proceeded, this time without distraction, to count the individual class members.

"Twenty five." Bernadette said aloud. There *was* one missing. Emily was gone.

****

This time there was no mistaking it. Her headlamp was going dead. Slowly it would fade out, and then brighten for a moment.

This newest development in Emily's predicament affected her like nothing else had. Now she could feel the walls closing in on her, breathing became difficult and her gasps for air came out rattled and raspy.

She got on her hands and knees. Sure that there could be only one way out, the tunnel continued to curve upward, away from the cavern. All she had to do was follow it. Sheer panic of being left behind, cold, hungry, and now without light, pushed her. All of the safety information that she had been taught fled from her mind. Getting out was all that consumed her.

The light dimmed again as she reached the curve ahead. It was a straight path as far as she could see. Calming herself as best she could, Emily looked back to her resting spot. Her favorite book as a child popped into her head. Pulling off one of her gloves she tossed it backward into the tunnel.

Hopefully if someone tried to find her, this trail of "breadcrumbs" would help them find her.

2

RESCUER

Bernadette felt suddenly weak. Doug had taken her away from the group to sit down, and offered her something to drink.

"I noticed that you hadn't eaten anything." He said pushing the bottle of water into her hand. "I'm going to gear up and go back in. Don't worry, we'll find her." His smile had been reassuring.

"I don't understand how? How could he have miscounted? She's been down there for two hours!" Her anger flared up.

All semester she had listened about how the Professor said he had never lost a student, never had anyone injured, never left anyone behind. She doubted that if she hadn't missed her roommate, that no one else would have.

"I don't think he would have if his full attention had been on the task at hand and not pre-occupied *someplace* else. Besides, Bern, this was really all my fault. I should never have let Emily go after me. It was a stupid thing to do." Bernadette stared up at Doug. Even in the sunlight he looked pale and drawn.

"Don't. Emily and I are as much to blame for this mess as anyone. What were we thinking?" Bernadette asked more to herself than to Doug.

Never wanting to be one of the silly superficial college girls she knew, Bernadette had still made some foolish decisions, making flirting, jealousy, spite, and envy a bigger part of her life than it had ever been before. Shrinking at the thought she had left her dearest friend behind, all because of the desire to impress the member of the opposite sex, made Bernadette cringe inwardly.

The sound of tires on gravel snapped her out of her self-pity and back to reality. Soon, a green truck could be seen parking behind the school vans. She got to her feet and stood next to Doug as a tall forest ranger climbed out of the cab. He took off his hat and rubbed his forehead with the back of his hand, then walked over to where Professor Stevens was talking to the cute blonde girl. The two shook hands and started to talk.

The men exchanged worried looks and glances back toward the cave entrance as they talked. Bernadette was too far away to hear much of their conversation. Doug still stood next to her and was also transfixed on this new development. Professor Stevens turned away from the ranger and headed back to where the rest of the class had gathered. All the students were now aware that one of their own was lost in the maze of tunnels.

Tim was seated nearby, leaning on a tree trunk, head in his hands. He had gone pale as a ghost when he heard that Emily had not come out after him. His reaction of her friend's disappearance helped ease some of the hostility that Bernadette was feeling for him.

"Everyone, please grab your things and load up." Bernadette shot to her feet. There was no force on earth that would move her until she knew Emily was okay. She walked over to the Professor who also looked as if he had aged a few years in the last few minutes.

"Professor!" He cut her off before she was able to say anything else.

"Please Bernadette. I have more than just one student to think about. Ranger Morison has offered to help Doug, and the two of them will be going in to find Miss Rivers. As for the rest of you, it's better to get safely down the mountain as soon as possible." Bernadette didn't have time to protest when the Ranger appeared next to them. He nodded politely at her and turned to Professor Stevens.

14

"Before you go Professor, I could use some additional information about the missing girl."

"Her name is Emily!" Bernadette barked at him. She was frustrated and angry, taking it out on him. Taking a deep breath she continued. "Emily Rivers. She's twenty-three, dark red hair and green eyes." Feeling helpless Bernadette would have droned on and on about her friend, but Ranger Morison just put a gentle hand on her shoulder.

"Don't worry Miss, we'll find your friend." The ranger was almost as tall as Doug, with jet-black hair and deep brown eyes. He was kind but assertive about the situation. "I'll radio down that we need an ambulance to meet us at the base of the mountain." He was now talking to Doug but Bernadette was not about to be dismissed so quickly.

"I'm not leaving!" She exclaimed emphatically.

****

The light flickered on one more time before sputtering out. Emily was swallowed up in blackness. She hit the helmet hard with the palm of her hand but nothing happened. It was dead.

The icy fingers of fear crept up on her again and forced her to close her eyes and envelop herself in the warm darkness that lay behind her eyelids. She had no way of knowing how far she had gone, and now with no light, she regretted leaving her original spot at all.

Just before the light had died she saw that the tunnel ahead forked. It had done the same a while back and she had taken the fork that seemed to slope upward to the right. She had left her second glove behind to mark her trail.

Emily, using her now bare hands as her only guide, patted the floor and walls while inching forward.

Reaching the fork, she said a silent prayer and turned left. Her helmet scraped along the low ceiling as she crawled. Soon the ceiling seemed to be pushing down on her as the space became smaller and smaller. Lying almost flat she tried to back out of her sandwiched state, out to the fork. It was harder in reality than theory.

Her body felt trapped; the lamp mounted to her helmet was making it hard to maneuver. She could feel small jagged rocks cutting their way through her pant legs and into her flesh. Emily wished she could push the hair out of her face, or stop beads of sweat that dripped into her eyes.

"Help!" The word slipped out, knowing that no one was out there looking for her. It was more a sob than anything else. Digging her toes into the loose gravel and planting her hands on whatever hard surface she could find, she pushed herself backward. Emily's shirt was forced upward by the movement and she winched as rocks with edges that felt like razors cut into the now exposed tender flesh of her stomach.

Slowly, as Emily began to realize that this was working, that the ceiling was retreating and she could now return to her hands and knees she let out a deep breath of sheer relief. Soon she had felt her way back to the fork. She sat for a time, licking her dry cracked lips, letting her heart rate slow down, and keeping her eyes closed to the blackness.

Emily was feeling very much like a child that is scared of the dark. She preferred the darkness created by her tightly closed eyes than the real one that lay thick all around her. For a long time she sat at the edge of the two tunnels, eyes closed. Beyond the impenetrable darkness was the deafening silence. The only thing she could hear was the sound of her own breathing.

It was an eerie feeling, being so isolated. She didn't like at all the affect it was having on her. Cold with sweat, tired and scared; the walls had started to close in on her.

16

This new sensation sent chills up her back. She had to keep moving or risk going mad in the nothingness.

Resolved, she headed up the opposite fork. It curved upward for a moment and then down, like a rocky rollercoaster. Then without warning the ground under her hands was gone. Air, musty, cold air filled the space. She had not reacted fast enough to keep herself from falling.

Nothing could have terrified her more than the fall into a deeper kind of inky blackness, the kind that swallows you whole.

Her head hit first, rocked hard inside the protective helmet. She felt as if her skull would split. The wind was knocked out of her as her ribs made contact with the hard, uneven surface. She heard, rather than felt, her ribs crack. The sound was deafening in the empty space.

****

Bernadette sat on the picnic table, watching Doug and Ranger Morison prepare to enter the caves. Each man carried rope, water, a first aid kit, extra lanterns, and other climbing gear that she didn't know the names of. She was left with her own pack, a few old blankets from the ranger's truck, and the one thing she hated most, time.

"We are going to retrace the group's steps. Hopefully Emily hasn't gone off the trail we took and it should be fairly easy to find her." Doug was talking to her but Bernadette only heard half of what he said. She nodded and looked into the mouth of the cave. Doug sat down across from her, blocking her view. He laid a hand over hers and smiled, "We'll be back soon." It was a promise. She smiled back at him a little and suddenly realized that he was touching her. The sensation was illuminating.

"I've left the cab of the truck open if you need anything. We'll have radios on us at all times but I am not sure how far these new ones will penetrate once we get into the cavern," Ranger Morison said, handing Bernadette the other radio and turning on his heel.

Doug squeezed her hand in farewell and took off after him. She watched the two men walk away from her, Doug running a hand through his hair before strapping on his helmet. The gesture seemed too normal for the situation, but soon both were gone, swallowed up by the mouth of the cave.

Alone, Bernadette felt she would go mad waiting for them, her mind racing with possibilities. She kept her eyes on the cave, hoping that soon she would see Emily come crawling out, dusty, shaken but no worse for the wear.

Memories flashed through Bernadette's mind. She and Emily had met their first day of College as roommates. Both young, inexperienced, away from home for the first time and ready to conquer the world. Freshman year of college had taught both of them valuable lessons in life, love, and most of all friendship.

Bernadette always felt that they complemented each other as friends very well. Emily was looking for family that would care about her and Bernadette missed the close relationship she had with her mother, who was states away.

With no one else to turn to the two of them had become fast friends. Now years later they were just as close as ever but for different reasons. Their friendship was now built on time, shared experiences, laughs, and hardships.

She looked down at her watch. Three and a half hours. Emily had been lost for three and a half hours. The minutes ticked on.

****

Emily lay motionless, her body bruised and sore. She wasn't sure if she had broken anything else but was afraid to move. Tears flowed freely down her face, not from fear, but from the pain of breathing.

Each time she drew a breath the broken rib protested the movement. Her head didn't hurt nearly as badly as she thought it should, but there were small white dots behind her eyelids when she closed them.

Not sure how far she had fallen, or if she would be able to get back up, despair set in. She felt sure that hours had gone by and there was no sign of anyone looking for her. Emily held on to the hope that Bernadette was rustling some feathers and if she knew her friend, Bern would be organizing a search party. The thought made Emily smile a little in spite of herself.

More time passed and Emily forced her eyes to stay open. Now exhausted, she knew she had to stay awake; with her head injury, concussion was possible and every time she closed her eyes her head began to swim.

"Stay awake." She said softly to the darkness. It was becoming harder and harder not to move. Lying on the uneven ground covered in rocks, her body had started to twitch and protest being in such an uncomfortable position. Biting down on her bottom lip she slowly moved her right arm out from under her and used it to push herself up a little.

The movement was excruciating and bile flooded her mouth. Before she could stop it she was hunched over as far as her body would allow her to go, stomach lurching, emptying itself out. She half cried, half wailed at the ground beneath her. Each retch was more painful that the one before it.

No longer able to stop the violent shutters that had overtaken her, Emily let out an ear splitting scream in-between gasping for air and the ever-present stabbing pains in her side. Her back arched into the air as dry heaves pushed their way up her body. She felt herself spinning, falling again, and rolling away on the cavern floor, the blackness suffocating her. Coming to rest on her left side, Emily laid staring, no more tears, no longer shivering, and no longer waiting.

Not sure how long she had been like that, so lost in her own mind, she didn't even seem to notice that the walls around her had started to dance with light. Shadows crawled the walls and were gone. She didn't notice that someone called her name. Sure that she was dreaming, the feeling of a hand on her face brought her back.

"Emily, my name is Kip; I'm here to help you." The voice was low and far away. Then a boot stepped into her line of sight and the stranger was kneeling down beside her. Then another voice cut into her solitude.

"Bernadette says to hurry up." It was a voice that she knew, Doug. At the sound of her friend's name, Emily began to sob.

3

ILLUMINATION

Bernadette wrung her hands together as she waited. She knew that hardly any time had passed, but being alone and not having any idea what was happening to her friend, made it feel like hours that turned into days.

She walked back and forth in front of the caves entrance, not wanting to sit. Nervous energy keeping her moving.

Birds sang in the trees, the warm sun touched her face with its light fingers through the green filters of the treetops. It could have been a very pleasant day but she saw nothing of it. Then just as Bernadette was sure she could no longer stand being left alone, off to her right she saw a golden beam of light hit the side of the cave.

"Hello?" She cupped her hands around her mouth and called into the nothingness. No one answered her. For a brief moment she was sure she had only imagined the light. But no! There it was again!

"Hello?" Again waited for an answer.

"Hello!" It was Doug's voice. Slowly the light faded as he came closer and was swallowed up by the bright sunlight. He stepped out and straightened. "We found her!" A grin spread across his face.

"Thank you!" Bernadette was so overcome with relief that she didn't seem to be thinking straight and flung herself at Doug. She wrapped her arms around his neck and kissed his cheek.

"Oh!" He stiffened under her touch, but his arms had encircled her as well and the warmth of it did not go unnoticed. She blushed and pulled back. His hands still rested at her waist.

"Sorry...I..." Bernadette could hear herself stammer and was unable to stop. She bit her bottom lip and slipped out from his arms. Letting her own arms drop back to her sides.

"Ranger Morison is with her now. He sent me back to get a few things." His words came out in a rush as if he was trying to bring back some of the normal tone to their interaction.

"Is she hurt?" Bernadette felt tears welling up behind her eyelids.

"It looks like a few broken ribs and she also took a pretty good bump to the head. Ranger Morison wants to get her as immobilized as possible before we can try to move her."

"Where is she? I mean, what happened? How did she get hurt?" Doug was moving now toward the Ranger's truck, and Bernadette was following close behind.

"Her light went out, she panicked, got lost down a small side passage, then fell off the edge of a cliff." He turned to Bernadette and something in his eyes told her there was more. "The fall wasn't very far. She landed on a small ledge. If she had gone just a few more inches to the side she would have fallen again, there was a second drop off... she was lucky! The second drop is more than thirty feet down." Doug said the last sentence in a low voice, his eyes searching for something on the horizon that Bernadette couldn't see. He seemed to be lost in thought for a moment before shaking his head and gathering up the items he had come back for.

"I'll be right back." Doug said and with long strides disappeared into the mouth of the cave once again.

****

Emily kept insisting that her head felt fine now, but the dark, handsome Forest Ranger would not let her sit up. He had placed a small lantern on the ground near her. Then went to work with something in his pack.

"Your friend will be back in a moment with a few things that we need, then we'll get you out of here. Try to be patient."

"I am!" Emily snapped at him. He was too calm, too in control for her. She was grateful that he had found her and more grateful that she would soon be out, but the pain in her ribs made her irritable.

"Was it your incredible patience that made you try to find your own way, without any light source?" Emily glared up at him for a moment until she saw the smile that played around his lips. He was joking with her.

"Okay, I'll give you that one. But tell me Ranger…"

"Morison."

"Ranger Morison, have you ever been lost in a cave? Lost without food, water, or light? You'll have to *forgive* me for panicking"

"Oh, I never said I thought that this was *all* your fault." He waved a hand over her. "Your teacher should have been better prepared with this many inexperienced students."

"You're right but I still feel stupid for moving this far alone."

"It helped that you left markers behind." He lifted one of her gloves from his pocket. "I was glad to find that you hadn't become too lost or we may have found you with nothing on." Ranger Morison lifted one eyebrow, his face illuminated by the glow of the lantern. He was smiling again. Unable to stop herself, she smiled back.

"I'm glad I can make your job more interesting… I am assuming you don't deal with a lot of glove dropping naked bears to keep you on your toes." He laughed, a laugh that made Emily want to join. She would have, too, if her ribs hadn't protested the act.

"I don't believe there is anything *much* wrong with your head after all." He chuckled.

"There wasn't before either… but after this I will have to invest in some night lights for a while." Emily was surprised at herself. Even with the pain in her sides she felt good, better now that there was light and that she was no longer alone. There was a sense of relief from the stress and fear that had held her in this place.

"I'll be sure to contribute to the night light fund." He winked at her. Emily was taken in by his dark eyes, his quick bright smile, black hair, strong jaw and overpowering good looks. Made more impressive by the lanterns glow casting shadows across his striking features.

She was also annoyed with herself for noticing any of it. But in such close proximity it was hard not to notice him. Even crouched next to her in the small space he was larger than life. He had wide strong shoulders, well-muscled arms, and, a few years younger, she would have guessed he had been a football player.

"You're quiet all of the sudden. No witty remark?" He asked. "Something on your mind?" His eyes narrowed and he leaned his arm on one of his legs, adjusting his stance.

"You mean besides my current predicament? Actually, I am surprised I can have a rational conversation let alone add any witty remarks."

"The humor *might* be a little out of place. I mean for the situation. You should really be in shock. I keep waiting for the signs…"

"Sorry to disappoint you, I was planning on going crazy later." Emily's words dripped with sarcasm.

"I'll be keeping my eye on you, just in case." Kip winked at her.

"Oh." Emily wasn't sure why but in spite of herself she hoped he would. She found herself studying Kip; he looked fairly young in the face; no lines or wrinkles on his smooth skin. "You're really easy to talk to... guys my age never really seem to be. Or, maybe it's me, and I am not easy to talk to?" She said almost absentmindedly.

"A little of both maybe." He agreed, still smiling. She frowned at him.

"What does that mean?" She asked feeling very much at a disadvantage laying on the ground and trying to carry on an intelligent conversation.

"Most *guys* would be intimidated." She let out what could have been the beginning of a laugh but was stopped by the shooting pain. She grimaced a little and tried to steady her breath.

"Intimidated?" She forced the word out with difficulty.

"It's intimidating talking to an attractive woman and you don't help the situation by pretending to be completely unaware of your affect on the opposite sex. So, yes, a little of both." Emily would have blushed at the half compliment, half accusation, but she was in too much pain to be either flattered or angry.

"Well it looks like our conversation will have to be carried on at a later time. Your friend has returned."

****

As Bernadette waited, the minutes that seemed like years, ticked by. Then both men emerged from the cave, holding between them an orange board that resembled a stretcher; Emily was on it. Bernadette rushed to her friend.

"Emily!" Her friend reached out a hand to Bernadette. "Are you okay? Are you hurt… very badly?"

"A few broken ribs that I know of for sure." Emily was taking shallow short breaths, to prevent more pain.

"Lots of cuts and I'm pretty beat up. Ranger Morison wants to keep me from moving, just in case, but, I don't think it's anything more…" She trailed off and closed her eyes. The strain was taking a toll on her. "I knew you would send someone for me." She whispered and a single tear streamed down the side of her face. The faith that Emily had in Bernadette touched her.

"Of course I would! I can't afford to rent an apartment all on my own and finding someone to pick up your end of the bills just seems like a lot of work right now." Both girls smiled at each other.

"I love you too." Emily said. Bernadette noted how pale and small she looked, strapped down, a neck brace helping to hold everything in place. They had been walking slowly to the Ranger's truck as they talked.

"Miss?" Ranger Morison broke into the conversation, leaning his head toward Bernadette to indicate he was talking to her.

"Brummond." She answered his question.

"Miss Brummond, would you mind opening the back doors? We need to lay down the back seat for your friend." Bernadette let go of Emily's hand and did as he asked. As she did, she noticed the crooked smile that passed between the Ranger and Emily.

With a little instruction, Bernadette was able to fold the back seat neatly into the floor of the cab and then stepped aside. Doug and Ranger Morison took great care laying Emily on the now flat surface and strapped the backboard securely to the floor. Once

Ranger Morison seemed satisfied that she was in place, he and Doug relieved themselves of their equipment. Bernadette stayed with her friend.

"I was so worried about you!" Emily tried to smile away Bernadette's fears.

"I was too." She said sheepishly. "It was scary... to be so alone." Emily closed her eyes.

Bernadette didn't know what to say to comfort her. She, herself, had no idea what had taken place in the caves while Emily was alone and she could hardly imagine the events that had transpired in those long hours.

Once the men had discarded their helmets and packs, Doug settled into the driver's seat. Bernadette was surprised to find that the tall Ranger had curled his long legs underneath him and placed himself in the back with Emily, holding her hand in his. She stood for a moment looking from him to Emily.

"I guess I'm with you." She said climbing into the cab next to Doug. The truck roared to life and slowly started it's descent off the mountain.

Bernadette half turned in her seat to look back at Emily. Ranger Morison was looking down at her with a look on his face that made Bernadette feel as if she was seeing something very personal and private. The feeling unsettled her a little; like she was the stranger, the outsider, looking in. But, it was more than that. Emily was returning the smoldering looks at the Ranger.

Bernadette, her lips set in a frown, turned and sat looking at the road for a long while. Emily had crushes before and Bernadette had seen her with those men, but it never looked like this. Bernadette wasn't sure why it should bother her that an attractive man found her friend, as dear to her as a sister, pretty and interesting. But, it did. Then a realization dawned on her. It wasn't frustration at the two of them; it was at herself! She wanted someone to look at her the way that Ranger Morison looked at Emily.

She knew that when the two of them were together, Emily was always the one that took the attention. She was easy going, pretty, smart and funny. Bernadette felt plain and dull in comparison. She was short and thicker around the middle. To tell the truth, thicker all around, not fat, or even heavy set, she had curves and muscle, but not the lean softness of Emily's frame. Bernadette also had dark, curly, and unruly hair that she secretly hated for not being smooth and shiny. She didn't have her mother's heavy Boston accent but she had her looks.

Bernadette stole a glance back at the couple in the back seat and breathed a sigh. Emily looked just awful, cut, dirty, black and blue. Still Bernadette felt she would very much like to trade places if someone, or more particular, the man seated next to her, would hold her hand and smile at her with the softness that she saw in the Ranger's dark eyes.

"Are you okay?" It was Doug talking to her. Bernadette turned to face the driver.

"What?" She said, lost in her thoughts.

"No one has asked you if you are okay. I mean…with the stress… I was just wondering." He said softly.

"Oh." Bernadette was glad for the conversation. It kept her mind off of *other* things. "Sure, I guess. I am glad to have Emily back. That was the worst part, the not knowing."

"I think she will be just fine in a few weeks. She'll have to take it easy for a while." Doug said, his voice reassuring.

"We were supposed to be moving into an apartment off campus in a week or so. Now, I am not sure. Maybe she'll go home to recover." Bernadette was talking more to herself than to Doug. She felt anxious and needed something to keep her mind occupied.

"I saved this for you." Doug said, and pulled out a candy bar from his pocket. "I noticed that you didn't eat anything with the others." He held it out for her to take. Bernadette smiled at his thoughtfulness and took the offering.

"Thank you. I forgot all about being hungry." Doug smiled over at her then turned his eyes back to the road. They were making slow progress, being careful not to jostle Emily.

Bernadette pulled the wrapper off the candy bar and started to take small bites without tasting them. From the back seat she could hear Ranger Morison asking Emily trivial questions, helping to keep her alert and awake.

Then just as she finished the last of the chocolate, a bend in the road revealed the waiting ambulance that would take Emily the rest of the way. Doug came to a slow stop next to the vehicle. Before Bernadette could react, the local EMT's had doors open and Emily was moved. Not once did Ranger Morison let go of her hand. She watched as both of them disappeared into the back of the white ambulance.

"I…um…Can he do that?" Bernadette turned to Doug. "Will they let him ride with her?" She was surprised that the door had been shut and the Ranger had not rejoined them.

"Looks like it." Doug said as he pulled onto the road behind the ambulance.

Finding herself alone again, with the object of her affection, made her feel ill at ease and she started to fidget in her seat.

"She'll be fine, you know?" Doug said looking at her from the corner of his eye. He must have interpreted her movements as worry. Bernadette felt silly and tried to sit still.

"Oh, I know." She couldn't come up with anything else to say and fell back into silence. It was maddening to her. Why wasn't she able to have a normal conversation with the man?

Then something very unexpected and wonderful happened. Doug reached over and folded his long fingers over her left hand that lay on the seat between them. She hadn't noticed that she had been drumming her fingers as he drove. Now her hand lay quiet in his and Doug did not pull his away. Bernadette felt heat rising into her face and tried to relax her suddenly tense posture.

Doug wasn't looking at her with the smoldering eyes the Ranger had used on Emily but the warmth of his hand on hers was more than enough to send her pulse racing.

****

Emily was glad the worst was now over. She hated being poked and prodded. She hated having x-rays taken and answering questions. Worst of all, she hated being embarrassed when the doctors and nurses would talk about her like she wasn't there.

"This the girl that got lost in the cave?" One would ask, the other would confirm. No one really looked at her. It was frustrating because she already felt like a fool.

But, now she was settled into her room for the night. The attending Doctor insisted on her staying overnight, worried about concussion and her broken ribs. But Emily was sure that it was more than that. She was calm, calmer than maybe she should have been.

She didn't feel any of the emotions she had while lost and alone. Panic or hysteria didn't seem possible or rational in her current situation.

A light tap at her door drew her attention and Emily looked up to see Bernadette peeking inside.

"Come in."

"I wasn't sure if you would be sleeping." Bernadette said apologetically.

Emily noticed that Bernadette was glancing around her room; *looking for someone,* she thought to herself, and decided to answer the unspoken question.

"Kip's not here." Emily smiled.

"Kip?"

"Ranger Morison. He is telling my parents the latest update." Emily rolled her eyes at the mention of her parents.

"So you two are on a first name basis now?" Bernadette lifted an eyebrow.

"He is very… nice." Emily said, stressing the last word.

"Oh, no doubt he is *very* nice." Bernadette said with a wicked smile.

"Stop!" Emily cried and pain shot across her face. "Don't… don't make me laugh… it hurts!" She held her hands to her sides and tried to stop shaking. Bernadette walked to the bedside.

"Sorry, Emily. I didn't mean to be funny."

"No… it's okay… I just keep forgetting that I can't laugh and take big breaths at the moment."

"So, what is the verdict?" Bernadette asked, pulling up a chair.

"Well the Doctor says that I have three broken ribs, cuts," she held up her bandaged palms, "So lots of rest and fluids." Emily said pointing to the IV in her arm. "A night's stay in the hospital just in case of concussion and then tomorrow we'll go over the do's and don'ts of broken ribs. I am sure it comes with some riveting reading material and study guide. I am in rapture while waiting."

"Well at least the pain meds haven't killed your sarcasm!"

"I do feel pretty good at the moment. Whatever the nurse keeps pumping into my IV line is great stuff!" Emily smiled.

"So, what about good old mom and dad? Will they be gracing the small town of Lovell, Wyoming, with their presence? I am sure a parade could be arranged." Bernadette smiled back. The girls had been friends long enough to know each other's families quiet well. Emily knew that Bernadette's mother and father were loving parents. They lavished attention on their only daughter. Bernadette knew that Emily's mother and father cared more for appearance and long extravagant get-a-ways, than their four children.

"To be honest, seeing as how I am not dying, I don't think they will cut their trip short. Kip... sorry Ranger Morison... was able to reach them and keep them abreast of the days events."

"Sorry."

"Don't be. I'm not a teenager any more wishing they would have at least come to see me in the play or help me pick out my dress for prom. They are who they are. Besides, I don't need anyone else to fuss over me. It's driving me nuts!" Emily complained in more detail about the nurses that talked about her, and not to her, and how they seemed to have nothing else to do but look in on her every five minutes.

"I could go run over someone in the parking lot and keep them busy if that would help?" Bernadette asked in a hopeful voice.

"Please do!" They both smiled.

"Well... I guess it's about time you got some sleep." Bernadette said and the sound of sadness that edged into her voice didn't go unnoticed by Emily.

"Are *you* okay?"

"Oh, Emily! I feel like an idiot! No, I don't want to talk about it. Trust me you have bigger problems right now." Pushing back the chair, Bernadette got to her feet. "I'll

32

be back early with some real food. I don't know how anyone can live on the stuff they serve in the hospital."

"Promise you'll tell me later what's on your mind?" Emily asked with real interest.

"Sure. But just get better first and then I'll fill you in." Bernadette walked to the door and stood, hand on the handle for a minute. She shook her head and looked back at Emily. "See you tomorrow." Emily felt that Bernadette had wanted to say more but was stopping herself. Before she could press her friend for more, Doug Arthur pushed the door open and half stepped inside the room.

"Hello." He smiled at Emily. "Are you ready?" This was addressed to Bernadette.

"Sure." Emily saw her friend blush a little under his gaze.

"See you tomorrow, Emily!" Doug said, waving a hand and holding the door open for Bernadette. She smiled sheepishly at Emily and walked out of the room.

So *that's* what was on her mind. Doug Arthur... Emily smiled a little to herself and let her eyes wander the room as she became lost in thought. It would be nice if Bernadette acted on her feelings for him, and they did look good together.

Before too long Emily closed her eyes. She was worn out, too much stress, coupled with physical exhaustion and, now pain medication. She drifted into sleep.

It only felt like minutes before someone was talking to her, breaking their way into her blanket of nothingness. She didn't want to open her eyes but the voice kept telling her to.

"Miss Rivers." It was a new nurse now; the room was dark and cold. Emily shivered a little then regretted doing so.

"Ouch!"

"Sorry to wake you. We have to check on you every two hours."

"All night?" Emily was not happy with this new development.

"Doctors orders. You hit your head pretty hard according to your friend over there." The nurse let her eyes wander to the right hand side of the small room. Emily's head followed in their direction and was more than surprised to see Kip Morison sitting in a faded old chair in one corner of the room. He had his head resting on the wall in back of him, hat pulled down over his eyes, legs stretched out and crossed at the ankles, arms folded across his chest.

Emily was awake now. If truth were told, she had not expected to see him again. He had no real connection to her. It had been nice of him to talk to her all the way down the mountain and fill the EMT's in on her fall and possible injures. But, she had not thought he would really stay with her. He had insisted that he help contact her family for her. Once that was done, Emily was sure he would have gone back up the mountain to work. Not camp out in her hospital room.

The nurse seemed to be done fiddling with whatever it was that she had been doing while Emily lay staring at Kip.

"Try and get some more sleep, I'll be back to check on you later." She smiled and left the room. Emily didn't know if she could sleep now. She wanted to, but her eyes wouldn't stop studying the sleeping man.

Slowly, she felt her eyelids growing heavy and her body melting into the soft mattress. It wasn't long before she was lost in dreams.

It started out simple enough. Emily stood in the middle of a field, green and sparkling in the warm sunlight. She knew she must be dreaming because her movements were slow and labored and it didn't hurt to breathe. She felt herself walking down a path; out of the field, then, without warning, the ground under her feet was gone. Emily was falling, her arms shot out to catch her, and her legs kicked in the emptiness. She could hear herself scream. Not again! The thought rang in her head. This did not feel like a dream. This felt real. Very, very real.

Emily gasped for air. She was still falling, faster now, into darkness. The light that had shown in the field was gone. Blackness, like ink, filled the space all around her. *No!*

"Emily!" There it was again, the same calm smooth voice calling to her. She had heard it before... in the cave. "Emily, it's okay." He was talking to her, touching her, a warm hand on her face, pushing back her hair. Emily opened her eyes.

"Kip." She said in a voice that sounded nothing like her own.

"It's okay. You're safe now." His deep voice was low. He was inches away from her, leaning over the bed rail. "It was just a dream." Still soothing her he brushed the back of his hand across her cheek. It was then that Emily realized he was wiping away tears.

"I thought... I thought I was fine." She said. "But then... then I was falling... falling all over again and I couldn't stop." She closed her eyes tightly to block out the memory.

"The more you hold it in the more it will eat away at you."

"But I don't want to be scared. I don't want to be weak. I feel so dumb for letting fear drive me, for getting lost."

"Emily, it's okay." Kip was still so close that Emily could breathe him in. She liked the way he smelled, earthy and strong. He had a strange affect on her; a comforting affect.

A nurse poked her head inside the door.

"Everything alright?"

"Bad dream." Kip answered. She nodded and left the room. He turned back to Emily with concern in his eyes. "Try and get some rest." She felt that he wanted to say more, but as she watched him, the kindness slipped from his face and his dark eyes grew cold. Kip took his hand away from her face and moved to sit back in his chair.

Hours later Emily still lay awake. Every so often she would pacify a nurse with answers to the never-ending questions as they checked on her, but Emily's heart was never in the conversation. She was fighting with herself, trying not to look at Kip, but losing the battle.

What had happened? He had been so nice to her, so caring, then suddenly he had changed. Had she done something wrong? He sat in the same position she had noticed him in earlier. *Sleeping*, she thought. Why wouldn't her mind calm down enough so she could also?

4

CALM BEFORE THE STORM

Tuesday May 13th

As promised, Bernadette arrived at the Lovell Hospital early the next morning. It had been a long night for her after leaving Emily. Doug had taken her home. It surprised her that she didn't have to tell him what dorm the girls lived in for the summer. He was more observant than she gave him credit for.

He was polite, walking her to the door and saying good night. She had watched him walk away and felt her heart fall a little, sure this would be the last time that she would see him outside of class.

Now she was back to pick up her friend and thoughts of Doug had to be pushed to the side. Bernadette knocked on the door and let herself in to the room. Emily lay in the hospital bed, just as she had the day before; but this time she looked more tired in a way that Bernadette wasn't able to explain; almost angry.

"Hi. So when do I get to break you out of this place?" She asked and placed a bag of fast food on the table next to Emily.

"The doctor wants to talk to me first." She half smiled at Bernadette. "But I have been ready for hours!"

"I'll bet. I don't like hospitals." There was another knock at the door and Bernadette turned around in time to see Ranger Morison walk into the room. It should not have been surprising that he was dressed the same way she had seen him the day before, but it didn't escape her notice that this uniform was wrinkled and his dark hair

37

uncombed. Bernadette caught Emily's eye and smiled when color came into Emily's cheeks.

"Good morning Ranger Morison." She said trying to get her smile under control.

"Please call me Kip. Nice to see you again."

"Oh, yes. I was just bringing Emily something to eat. Would you join us?" Bernadette found great pleasure in the look of discomfort that played across Emily's face.

"I have to get back, I just wanted to say good bye." This was not directed at Bernadette and she stepped to one side. "I hope you feel better soon." She could tell that there was much left unsaid between the two.

"Thank you." Emily smiled at him. He turned to leave and was almost out the door when Bernadette found her voice.

"Ranger! Kip, I mean." He turned back. "Emily and I are moving into a new place and well… with so many of our friends gone for the summer… and Emily being hurt…I was wondering if you could help? With some of the heavier boxes?" Emily gasped behind her. Bernadette was trying hard to give him her most pleasant smile.

"Sure." He was looking beyond her again to Emily.

"I'll give you our number and address. That way we can coordinate." Bernadette was now talking more to herself, she knew, jotting down the information on a napkin she handed to him. "It's really nice of you to help us. Thanks."

"My pleasure."

"Yes, thank you." Emily was blushing just a little as he took his leave. Once alone, Bernadette turned on her friend.

"So, what happened?"

"I don't know what you mean." Emily tried to keep a straight face and Bernadette could tell she was lying.

"He didn't stay all night did he? I mean he looked like he did. Did he?" She watched as Emily's eyes wandered to an old chair. "He did!" Bernadette shouted.

"Shhhh! Yes, he slept in the chair. It was kind of sweet. But I don't know."

"Don't know what? I think he kind of likes you and if I hadn't stepped in to ask him to help, you would have let him go without another word."

"That was the plan."

"Why? Emily, he is very handsome and he seems very nice."

"He seems nice, sure, but… Oh, I don't know."

"Something happened! Tell me." Bernadette demanded and reached for the food. As they ate Emily told about her nightmare, their closeness, and then his strange reaction to it. Before Bernadette could comment on it, Emily was asking her a question.

"So, your turn. What happened with Doug?"

"Nothing… well not nothing, he did hold my hand for a while. But nothing really."

"Is that what was bothering you last night?" Emily asked.

"Yes. I feel really confused around him. It didn't help that I was alone with him either, and I never know what he is thinking. He doesn't look at me with dark eyes like your ranger." But their conversation was cut short as the Doctor entered the room.

"Broken ribs are a unique healing challenge. The rib cage moves with each breath and we really can't do much to help immobilize your ribs. So, I am going to prescribe plenty of rest. You need time to heal, and resting will put less strain on your ribs.

"I want you to use your pain medication, too. Don't try to be a martyr. You can also use cold packs or heat, if you would like. I will be sending you home with a chest binder to help protect the ribs.

"Most of all Miss Rivers, be patient. Three broken ribs will take time to heal. No sports, lifting, twisting, things like that. Here is a list of other things to avoid. After you are dressed and ready to go, one of the nurses will go over some breathing exercises to help while recovering." He talked fast, not once looking up from his chart. It almost seemed to Bernadette that he was just going through the motions and not concerned for the person in front of him. Then, he was gone and a nurse was pushing her way in.

"Whenever you are ready to dress just let us know and we'll get you out of here."

****

Later that afternoon Bernadette found herself alone walking across campus, a tray of food in her hands. Emily was in their dorm room reading a book and Bernadette had offered to grab them some lunch from the cafeteria.

"Bernadette!" She heard her name but wasn't sure in what direction it had come from. Then from the other side of the clock tower Doug stepped into view. He was waving at her.

"Hi." She said as he came closer.

"How is Emily?" He asked as he stopped in front of her. Bernadette knew that it shouldn't bother her that he was asking about her roommate but it did, just a little.

"Fine, I am just about to feed the invalid." She said holding out the tray of food.

"Can I walk with you?" He asked and took the tray out of her hands.

"Um… Sure." They walked without saying anything. Then just across the street from her dorm building, Doug stopped. He was standing in front of the administration building. For a moment Bernadette didn't notice he was no longer next to her. She turned to see him placing the tray on a nearby bench. He walked over to her, something unreadable in his expression. Under the shade of the trees, he looked down at her.

"There is something I wanted to do, that I should have done, but last night you looked... so stressed I didn't want to add to it." He was talking but Bernadette couldn't seem to follow a thing he was saying.

"Doug?" It was just in that instant that he took her hand in his. He pulled her off to the far side of the sidewalk near a light pole. Now he was closer to her than before.

"I'm going to kiss you now." He said softly, but with so much authority that it stopped Bernadette from talking. Then he did kiss her, bending down to do so. He took her face in his hands and looked deep into her eyes. The kiss was soft and sent shivers down her spin. Doug was kissing her and she was standing there, arms at her sides, eyes wide open, looking around her and feeling so many things all at once.

He stopped when Bernadette didn't seem to respond to him and pulled back to look at her. She was staring at him.

"I'm sorry. I shouldn't have done that."

"No!" Bernadette had found her voice. "No, I'm glad you did." She said, quieter now. She was suddenly aware of everything around her, the summer sun shinning down through the trees, the birds singing, the way she trembled under his gaze, and, the taste of his lips. Everything seemed to be brighter, newer, somehow.

Bernadette slipped her fingers around Doug's neck and kissed him back. He responded in a way that she hadn't been able to. Holding her close, one hand tangled in her hair, Doug was kissing her. Bernadette couldn't stop smiling and a laugh bubbled it's way up and she had to pull back to let it out.

"Laughing is always what you want to hear when you kiss a girl." Doug said with a disgusted look on his face.

"No, I'm not laughing at you! I'm just laughing at... myself, I guess."

"I don't think I follow." He still held her in his arms.

41

"I've just…well the truth is… I have liked you for a long time, but I was sure you had no idea who I was." It was Doug's turn to laugh. His low chuckle warmed Bernadette from the toes up. When he looked back into her eyes, his own were soft and warm.

"I practically begged you to take a summer class just so that I could be closer to you. Didn't you notice?" Bernadette hadn't really, just thinking he was excited about a class he loved. "So many times I would place myself so that if you needed a question answered, or a partner, you would pick me. It was maddening to me that Emily always stole your attention.

"She is a nice girl but she didn't make getting to know you any easier, without making a fool of myself in front of the whole class. I was glad when the two of you wanted to change partners yesterday." He stopped for a minute and traced the line of her jaw. "I am sorry Emily was lost and hurt."

"Oh." Bernadette wasn't sure she could speak so freely about her own feelings.

"What are you thinking?"

"I am sad you didn't kiss me last night." She smiled at him, blushing. "I took the class just to be around you." It was the truth and she hoped he could see that.

"We're a sad pair." He was still smiling down at her. With an arm around her waist, he steered her back to the tray full of food. "I know you have to help Emily, but I would really like to see you later."

"Yes." Bernadette didn't want him to leave.

"I'll drop by." He was picking up the tray and turning his steps back in the direction of her dorm. Bernadette followed. Too soon they were once again standing in front of her door. "Tell Emily I hope she is feeling better." He said, but the smile on his face was only for Bernadette.

"I will." She reached for the tray and as she took it from him he leaned over and kissed her lightly on the check.

Bernadette floated into her room and shut the door. She could feel herself blushing, still. Turning to face Emily, she let the smile she had been holding back spread over her face, her body slumping against the door for support.

"Bernadette?"

"He kissed me." She said simply. Understanding dawned on Emily's face.

"Tell me everything!" She squealed and the two friends soon forgot all about the tray of food.

****

Eight Weeks Later

Monday July 7th San Diego, California

Harold Pinchly bent over his computer, his eyes bloodshot after hours staring at his screen. His fingers cramped but Harold refused to stop pounding away at the keys.

"Still plugging away are we?" Harold jumped at the sound of the voice then trying to look as nonchalant as possible lifted his head and gave the fellow co-worker a nod.

"Don't work to hard Pinchly." The other man smiled and walked to the elevator.

Harold pushed back his reading glasses from the tip of his nose. Sweat dripped down the back of his neck and trickled between his shoulder blades. He nervously punched his mouse, clicking open a file that was deeply imbedded into his computer's hard drive. Pages and pages of numbers appeared, scrolling past. Harold wasn't sure if it was because of all the time he had spent copying the information and translating it into code but the longer he looked at the numbers, patterns started to form.

He shook his head, trying to clear his mind. It was now or never. Harold pressed the download icon and held his breath as the files were copied onto a portable flash drive. He wouldn't be able to erase all his tracks and he was positive that within hours of someone noticing his sudden disappearance the wolves would be at his door.

Harold picked up the photo of his daughter resting on the table and brushed his thumb across the clean glass. He prayed that keeping her out of the loop would help keep her safe.

His computer beeped and Harold quickly removed the drive. Then set to work erasing or corrupting any files left. He watched as the virus ate away at his work. It was time.

5

TIME HEALS ALL WOUNDS

The ribs had healed nicely in the past two months with the help of Acetaminophen for the pain and all outward signs had long since been wiped away. The only constant reminder of her ordeal were the images and feelings she had when she closed her eyes. Sleep did not come easily, and, even now, Emily sometimes felt the need for a prescribed sleeping aid to push the nightmares aside. It wasn't helping.

But in the weeks that followed Emily's fall in the mountain cave she had something else that also pressed on her mind. Kip Morison. The tall ranger had held her hand all the way down the mountain. He had stayed by her side in the hospital, called her parents and been a comfort to her.

Emily wondered about him, that first night in the hospital when she had stayed for "observation". Kip had made himself comfortable in an old faded chair in one corner of her room.

The memory brought feelings bubbling up that Emily was at a loss to explain. He was quiet, reserved, but always aware of what was going on. The image of Kip being with her was fading into the background.

He was there when the girls moved into their apartment off campus a few days later and refused to let Emily do more than unpack her personal items. His quiet strength made her feel safe and comfortable. She didn't feel the dependence on medication when he was around, yet when he left, she felt the darkness of the cave crushing her again.

It didn't occur to her that she could be feeling more for him then she wanted to, until the last time she saw him. Letting her mind rush back in time she played the memory like a movie in her head.

Six weeks after coming home from the hospital, Bernadette wanted to have a party to show off their apartment. Many of their college friends were returning from their summer travels and would be able to attend.

It was a warm summer day, a light breeze played on the air, and Emily had been gazing at Kip from under her eyelashes for hours.

"Hey, Girly!" Bernadette bounced next to Emily. She was smiling, something she did a lot, as of late. Emily knew that it had something to do with all the time that Bernadette was spending with the object of her affection, Doug. They had come together after Emily's accident, and were now almost inseparable.

"Hey guys." Emily mumbled back. "What are the two of you up to?"

"Nothing much, just talking about whether Doug is going to go back as Professor Stevens TA or not."

"I don't feel right about going back after... after what happened last time. Stevens has someone else already lined up for the summer semester anyway."

Emily was listening to Bernadette and Doug but her eyes were on Kip working at the grill.

"Go talk to him!" Bernadette pushed her a little in the direction of Kip. "You know you want to!"

"I do." Emily admitted. "But I am not sure he wants to talk to me. He always seem so...severe... when I talk to him."

"Brooding. I think that's what they call it." Bernadette frowned a little. "He must like you a little... it's not me that he comes to see all the time." By this time Doug had joined them, he placed a hand around Bernadette's back pulling her to his side. Emily smiled a little, she was glad for her friend's happiness.

"Go." This time it was Doug that was encouraging her. Emily took a deep breath, took a plate and headed toward Kip, who was at the moment manning the grill.

She forced a smile and said. "What's good?" Kip looked pleased to see her.

"What would you like?" He asked turning over a hamburger.

"Oh… um I am not too hungry, so a hot dog."

"Did you want a bun too?" He asked, a playful look on his face. She looked down at her empty plate and smiled more easily this time.

"I guess I should have thought of something better to use as a cover." She mumbled and put the plate down.

"I'll let it slide this time." He smiled, a smile that went all the way to his dark eyes and it gave Emily courage.

"Bernadette really went all out for this party didn't she?" He asked looking around at their small back yard, full of summer decorations, lights, and streamers.

"Yes, she lives for this kind of stuff." Emily wished she still had the openness of their first conversation. But in the past weeks she had become more and more unsure of what to say when talking with Kip.

She felt drawn to him and enjoyed his company, but from time to time she would say something or look at him and all friendliness was gone. He would shut down. It was becoming very confusing to her. Emily wanted to ask him why, but never dared.

"Looks like things are winding down on the grill front." Kip said taking the last of the hot dogs and hamburgers from the grill.

"I'm not really in the party mood, would you like to take a walk with me? Northwest's campus is really pretty this time of year." Emily felt bold and hoped that he wouldn't say 'no'.

"Sure, lets grab some drinks." She had been rewarded. Kip went over to the cooler and pulled out two root beer sodas. He met Emily at the edge of the yard.

She saw Bernadette looking at the two of them as they walked away and smiled back at her. Bernadette gave her a thumbs up and Emily rolled her eyes in return.

"Things look almost the same from my time at the college. At that time Bridger Hall was still standing."

"I remember hearing about the fire on the Billings news, I wasn't in Powell when it happened." They walked across the street toward the music building, both sipping on drinks, and, neither talking.

Emily looked around at the place that had been her home the last few years. The small community college was pretty with red brick buildings and manicured lawns. After Graduating with an Associates Degree, Emily had stayed and taken correspondence courses from the University of Wyoming. She had also continued to take classes at the smaller Northwest College. Now that her last year was drawing to an end, she felt sad at leaving.

Lost in her own thoughts she hadn't heard Kip talking to her.

"Sorry, what did you say?"

"I was just wondering what your plans are for the fall?" He was being polite, she could tell.

"More school. I have another year before I graduate with my Bachelors in Education. After that I am not sure."

"Will you teach?" He asked.

"Right now my goal is to work with children with special needs in alternative classes."

"Really? That sounds great." Kip did sound impressed.

"I grew up working summers at a camp geared toward children with disabilities. I spent some of the best times of my life in Red Lodge, Montana with those kids. I fell in love and now I can't see myself doing anything but that. Did you always want to be a Forest Ranger?"

"Not always. I did spend a lot of time in the Big Horn Mountains as a kid but it wasn't until I was half way through college that I had made up my mind. I grew up at the foot of the mountains." She looked up at him. His black hair rustled a little in the summer winds. He was smiling to himself. "I didn't expect to love the job as much as I do. For the most part it's pretty tame, but every so often someone like you hands me a challenge." He was still smiling but looked over at Emily now. She smiled back.

"Sorry, couldn't help myself." They had turned down a new sidewalk now and once again fell into silence. Emily didn't mind so much now, Kip wasn't closed off and cold, and she enjoyed talking to him, no matter the subject. He started up the conversation again and the exchange seemed effortless and easy, both asking questions of the other so that soon they where sharing life stories and laughing.

Time slipped by, and before either was aware of it, dusk had fallen. Emily noticed that they were headed back toward her apartment and she felt her heart fall. She was having a great time and wasn't ready for it to end. There was also a feeling of apprehension. This was the most time she had spent alone with Kip in weeks.

"I had a great time." She said hopefully.

"I did to." Kip said smiling down at her. Emily felt herself blush a little under his gaze.

49

They were at her door sooner than she had thought possible and Kip stopped walking. He was leaving and Emily rushed to stop him.

"Would you like to come in?" She stepped closer to him in the dim light.

"I better let you go, tell Bernadette and Doug thanks for a great time." He didn't seem to notice her closeness and was looking away from her.

"Kip, wait." Emily felt a rush of confidence. "I… was wondering if…" Then in an action that took both of them off guard she reached out and touched his hand. "Maybe you would like…"

He cut her off. "No, Emily." Kip jerked away his hand. "I was hoping that it wouldn't come to this."

"I'm sorry?"

"Emily, I like you, I do. But I'm not at a point in my life… it's not right… I can't do this… no, you are so young…" He seemed to be having some difficulty with forming his thoughts into words. Kip turned toward her and the look in his eyes told her more than his words. He had shut off again.

"No, I get it." She backed up, heels hitting the bottom porch step.

"Don't be like that. I would like to stay friends." His dark look seemed to fade just a little as he talked.

"Friends? Right. Sorry Kip but I am not that dumb. I may be younger than you and have a little less life experience but I know full well what 'being friends' means." She was rambling, trying to cover the hurt she felt at being rejected.

"You came over every weekend on your days off." Emily went on. "You called, you stayed for dinner? Was I just a game? I don't understand. One minute we're on the couch watching a movie and you let me put my head on your shoulder and the next you can't look me in the eyes." Emily raged at him, she was angry recalling tender moments that had meant something to her. "I thought… I thought…" She had to stop, tears of anger and frustration brimming in her eyes.

"Emily." Her name on his lips was nothing more than a whisper. For a second she was positive he was leaning closer to her about to reach out a hand to comfort her, when without another word she watched him walk away, get into the cab of his truck and drive away.

Emily shook off the memory and blinked her eyes a few times. The tears had returned to them; she knew she had not just imagined all the little things that had passed between them. The times Kip had protectively placed a hand in the small of her back to lead her through a doorway. The time he had brushed hair out of her face when tussled by a warm summer wind, the tender look in his eyes when he thought she was not looking. No, it had all been very real, but now, she knew it had only been real for her.

Emily sighed. She had to get him out of her head, to live in the here and now and stop wondering what Kip was doing.

"Hey, I am going to the store to grab a few things for this weekend. You want to come?" Bernadette asked popping her head inside Emily's room.

"No, I wanted to take a shower and hop into bed." Emily tried to smile at her friend.

"Okay, I'll be back soon." Bernadette left and Emily waited to hear the front door close. Once she was satisfied that enough time had gone by, Emily grabbed the large pill bottle out of the nightstand drawer.

The pain prescription was old and deep down she knew she didn't need it, but she wanted it. It helped to dull all her feelings, not just the physical ones. Emily walked into the small kitchen and grabbed a bottle of water out of the fridge, then pulled off the lid from the prescription bottle. She poured two pills into the palm of her hand. Somewhere between placing them in her mouth and pulling the cap off the water she caught a glimpse of herself in the glass fronts of the kitchen cabinets.

"You don't need them, you know? Not for the ribs, not for the nightmares you're having, and not for... for..." She stopped herself from completing the sentence, as she looked closer into the reflection. The bitter taste of the pills slowly dissolving in her mouth made her feel sick and she rushed to the sink, spitting them out. Emily grabbed the bottle and dumped the remaining pills down the garbage disposal. Suddenly she felt ashamed and weak. Yet she was glad that the crutch she had been holding on to was now out of reach.

****

Tuesday July 15th

Rainer's piercing blue eyes narrowed into a slit. His thin lips pulled back into a sneer, one designer shoe dug into the soft flesh just beneath it. The middle-aged man pinned to the ground beneath Rainer's foot was sweating in the summer sun, beads trickling down and pooling around his head.

"Please!" He begged, chest heaving. "Please I don't know anything else!" Rainer was annoyed. He didn't answer the mans plea and pushed harder at his throat, then as if it was the most normal thing to do Rainer went about straitening his silk tie. Glancing with approval at his refection in the shop window. His hair glistened in the sun; long lean muscles flexed under hand-sewn fabric. The suit was new and it annoyed him that it was getting dusty and worn.

It annoyed him even more that a simple two or three day job was taking this long. Pinchly had led them on a wild goose chase and now here Rainer stood, in the back of a car rental building, under the glare of the sun, terrorizing some nameless man for information.

"I don't have time for this. Kill him." Rainer said as casually as if he had just ordered dinner not a man's death. Ulric's flame tattoo pulsed as his neck flexed. Rainer removed his foot and pulling out a handkerchief wiped away a speck of dirt from the neatly polished toe. Then stepped into the shade and pulled out a pair of sunglasses.

"No! Please! He left this morning, rented a car with cash. He didn't use the name Pinchly! Smith, that's what it was, Smith! He was headed toward Billings. Please!" The man begged for his life. Rainer knew he was telling the truth. Pinchly would be running out of options now. He was too far away from Denver to drive without being caught and now he had only one way out.

Pinchly had been planning this for some time. Paying all in cash, taking the long way around, changing his name from town to town. He even was smart enough to have a few fake ID's made. He had to give the old man some credit, not too much, because in the end Rainer always won. He had never once left a job unfinished.

Ulric cracked his knuckles and inwardly Rainer winched. He would never admit that the large man's appearance and affinity for deadly toxins bothered him. In the end Ulric got the job done and done well. Rainer couldn't argue that point. He turned on his heel, walked back to the sleek black SUV and slid into the back seat.

There were no more cries for pity, no more please for help. Not even a cry of pain but Rainer knew that the man was dead. Seconds later Ulric opened the opposite door and slid inside. Rainer wrinkled his nose at the sight of a small silver colored syringe as it was placed back into a leather pouch and rolled up along with others. Ulric tucked the pouch carefully into a small black bag and sat it in the seat between them.

"Poor man had a heart attack." Ulric said with laughter in his voice. The sound filled the interior of the SUV. Rainer nodded.

There was a mutual kind of respect between the two men. Although Rainer was more of a contractor than a killer, he was as lethal and deadly as the liquid slashing around in the vials Ulric carried and they both knew it.

"Lets go. We have some planning to do." Rainer ordered as the SUV's pulled back onto the road, leaving the small nameless town behind. He sat back, looked at his watch and lit a cigar.

6

FRIGHT OR FLIGHT

The alarm clock had gone off too early and Emily pushed the snooze button then rolled away from the telling red numbers.

There was a loud knock at the front door and Emily jumped.

"Yes?"

"Time to go ladies! You are going to be late." Emily recognized Doug's voice. She rolled back over and looked at the clock again, then shot out of bed. She must have gone back to sleep and now they would be cutting it close.

"Bernadette! Come on we only have ten minutes to get ready!" Bernadette lay in bed, the covers over her head. Emily pulled them back. "Come on!" Her roommate reluctantly rolled off her mattress.

"I'm up, I'm up." The knock at the front door sounded again.

"Is it safe for me to come in yet?" Bernadette looked down at her tattered pajamas, cringed then flung herself at the door.

"NO! I mean, just wait a minute…" Emily could hear Doug give a low chuckle. He had wanted to give Bernadette a ride to the airport but work had prevented him. He had still insisted on coming by to see his girlfriend off.

"Sleep in did you?" He called in a playful voice.

"How do I look?" Bernadette asked while she stood in front of the full-length mirror, she was trying to pin her dark hair back into a messy bun and do her makeup at the same time.

"Great! We have two minutes left…" There was another knock at the door.

"Ready?" Doug sounded amused on the other side. Bernadette visibly jumped at the sound of his voice. Emily picked up Bernadette's bags and tossed a pillow under one arm.

"You look great. Really! Now come on. We have to go."

"My tickets!" Bernadette sounded panicked for a moment and was ready to shoot back into her room to rummage for them when Emily grabbed her by the arm.

"You are picking them up at the ticket counter, remember? What would you do without me?"

"Never make it anyplace on time, that's for sure." Both girls rushed out the door.

"I'll put your things in the car while you say… goodbye." Emily winked at Bernadette then turned and left the two standing on the sidewalk.

Over the last week Emily had started to feel better about Kip not calling or dropping by like he had before. She still missed seeing him but was working very hard on keeping him out of her mind. Yet, at times like this, being the third wheel, she did miss him more than she would like to admit.

Placing Bernadette's things in the car she slipped behind the drivers seat and turned the car on. She tried hard not to notice the two exchange one last hug, or how Doug held onto her hand just a little bit longer before opening the door. Emily took a deep, relaxing breath.

"See you later Emily." Doug bent down and smiled at her as he shut the door. Then he leaned in the open window, and kissed Bernadette.

"Sure, see ya." Both girls put on their seat belts and then Emily pulled away from the curb. In her rear view mirror she could see Doug standing on the sidewalk until the car turned the corner.

"He wanted to know if you would be okay with him coming to pick me up after the family reunion? I said I didn't think you would care." Bernadette was talking while tossing trash out of her purse into a small plastic bag.

"I don't mind. I know you'll only be gone for four days but it seems like it's going to be harder on him than on me." Emily said, humor in her voice.

"Ha, ha, you are *so* funny." Bernadette glared at Emily then went back to picking old candy bar wrappers out of her purse.

****

The drive to Billings took less time than either girl expected and soon they were wandering around the Logan airport parking lot looking for a parking place.

"I've never seen the airport this full before." Emily said, more to herself than Bernadette.

"Oh! There's one!" Bernadette said, pointing to a car that was backing out. "Get it, get it!" She squealed as Emily raced to fill the space before someone else had the chance.

"Nice." She said and turned the car off. "Alright, let's go." Emily helped Bernadette gather her things and they rushed inside.

"I have to go grab my tickets, hold this for a sec." Bernadette said, tossing Emily her now half empty purse, then bent down over her bag to stuff the small bit of clothing back in place and pull the zipper up. She then took back her purse. "I'll be right back, stay here." She didn't wait for Emily to answer but dashed away, purse and bag in tow.

Emily waited for her near the exit doors, still holding Bernadette's pillow. She liked to watch people as they passed by her. Some carried young children; others went by in wheel chairs. At times the crowd of people would thin and Emily could make out Bernadette waiting in line at the ticket counter.

Then as she gazed over the crowd, not really looking at anyone in particular someone bumped into her as they rushed past, hard enough to make Emily lose her balance. She started to fall forward a little when the stranger reached out to steady her.

"Oh, I am so sorry miss!" Emily regained her footing and looked over at the older gentleman. He was dressed in a tattered suit, balding, bearded and sweating like it was one hundred and six degrees inside the air-conditioned building.

"No problem." Emily smiled at him. He didn't smile back as he let go of her arm, but, instead, looked over his shoulder, and then scanned the surrounding area. Emily wondered if he could be looking for someone and asked. "Are you lost, or meeting someone? Can I help?" He looked tired, like he hadn't slept in days.

"Looking, yes, but desperately trying to avoid." He shook his head. "No, I don't need any help, but thank you." He said rushing past her. Emily watched the strange man as he slipped into line a few people behind Bernadette.

Once Bernadette had her ticket she rushed back to Emily.

"I don't have very long before I have to go." She pushed back a stray hair that had forced its way out of the haphazard hair-do. "We really cut this close." Bernadette said eyeing her ticket.

"Well, let's say goodbye now so you don't miss your flight." Emily said, hugging her friend.

"Do you want me to bring back anything from Las Vegas?"

"Sure, I could use a million dollars! Play one for me." Emily slipped Bernadette a quarter and smiled.

"You know they don't play with change anymore." Emily pushed the pillow into Bernadette's hands and turned her around, pointing in the direction of the security checkpoints and escalators.

58

"Have fun!" Emily called out as she waved at her. Emily noticed that Bernadette was just behind the older man that had run into her earlier. Once again he was glancing around, wringing his hands together and looking very nervous. Emily wondered who it was that he was trying so hard to avoid, his wife, his ex, or maybe someone he had stolen money from? She let her mind play with the possibilities for a minute, and then smiling to herself she turned around and started for the doors.

Before Emily could walk two steps she came face to face with Kip Morison.

****

Bernadette turned and smiled at her friend, lifting a hand and waved over the crowd. Emily called out. "Have fun." Bernadette noticed that someone in front of her caught Emily's attention. Bernadette turned back around to see who Emily could be looking at and spotted a man just in front of her, suit looking a bit too big and worn. He was wringing his hands together and glancing around with eyes that darted.

Bernadette turned back to face the direction of her friend, but the crowd of people rushing to make their planes had thickened and she was nowhere in sight.

"Why is this taking so long?" A large woman next to Bernadette wailed at a nearby transport security officer that was walking past the forming line of people. He smiled over at her, but didn't stop to talk.

Someone else behind her pushed forward with greater impatience, and like dominos everyone fell forward a few steps into the people in front of them.

"Sorry." She muttered and glared back at no one in particular. Then she saw who must have been causing the ruckus. In the far corner of the crowd stood a large man towering over the heads of everyone around him.

Bernadette shivered involuntarily at the sight of him. He was imposing, taller than anyone she had ever seen in real life. It wasn't only his height that made him a spectacle. He was well muscled, like a bodybuilder, and showed off his large arms by dressing in a black tank top.

The giant sported a short military haircut, white like fresh snow. One eye was dark, the other, white as his hair. These attributes alone would have caused a certain amount of staring and pointing but the large man had added tattoos to his neck and arms. Then, like something normal people would have only seen in movies, the stranger also had one long angry red scar that marred his left arm.

"Wow." She heard the plump woman say, who also had caught sight of the tall stranger, as had most of the people around her. Then Bernadette felt his gaze land on her. For a second she couldn't look away.

Something over her shoulder caught his attention and he smiled, no, not smiled, leered. The strong jaw and stone face becoming something more strange and ugly.

Bernadette forced herself to turn around and walk the two steps forward as the gap between her and the old man became wider. It took all her willpower to keep her eyes in front of her. She studied the old man instead. He hadn't seemed to look back over the heads of the others to the giant. No, the old man was looking forward.

Then more suddenly than Bernadette could have thought possible, the towering man was standing next to her. She was surprised at how fast he could move and how quiet he had been. He didn't seem to notice her, but placed a large hand on the shoulder of the man in front of her.

The old man jumped a little, but by the time he turned around the giant was gone. Bernadette, still stunned by the giant's sudden appearance, then just as sudden his disappearance, she stared after him for a moment as he walked away. The crowd parted as he left.

"Oh my!" The women gasped bringing Bernadette's attention around from the giant; she glanced around to see what was now causing so much trouble. The older gentleman standing in front of her was now shaking with such violence that she wasn't sure how he was still standing. His eyes looked wild and dashed back and forth.

"Sir? Is something wrong?" Bernadette asked just as the old man stumbled away from her. Unable to keep her eyes from following him, she watched as he staggered toward the doors. Something else caught her eye as she followed his path through the airport. Emily was standing with her back towards Bernadette, talking to Kip Morison. There was a kind of uneasiness about his stance and the look on his face.

Bernadette knew Emily must have been surprised and none too pleased to have run into Kip and before she knew it her feet had moved. She felt a sinking feeling in the pit of her stomach and wanted to come to the aid of her friend, rescue her from the conversation. She dashed forward. Kip nodded toward Emily and stepped away, pushing his way out the doors.

****

Emily watched as Kip left her behind. She should be used to the feeling that always formed in the pit of her stomach at the sight of Kip walking away, but she wasn't. This time she wasn't given any time to wallow in the feeling, because, before she knew what was happening she was tackled from behind and knocked to the floor. Emily's right knee hit hard on the ground, jarring her.

"What?" She turned to see who it was that had accosted her.

"Please." The same man that had bumped into her earlier grabbed at her as he sank onto the floor. Emily reached out to steady him but collapsed with the old man in her arms. "Please" He said again, his words coming out gurgled, like he was chocking. It

61

was then she noticed a small drop of blood that had stained his suit. The old man shook again.

"What can I do?" She asked, scared.

"No cops!" He almost yelled up at her from his position on the floor, his eyes wide. Then he coughed a little and redness appeared in the corners of his mouth.

"Okay! It's okay." She said, touching his cheek, trying to be comforting. Behind her someone was yelling to call 911 and people were gathering.

"No cops! Trust no one. I'm so sorry!" His breathing was becoming labored and raspy. Coughing again brought more blood this time and it spilled down his face. Now terror shown in his eyes and Emily was sure it was reflecting in her own face. He was dying in her arms.

"Keep it safe, *Judith*, keep it safe!" It was a command. The old man reached up and grabbed one of Emily's hands, with his free hand he reached into his shirt pocket and pulled something small out. Depositing it into her hand he folded her fingers over it. "No matter what, keep it safe, *Judith*." His hand dropped from hers, leaving blood dripping off her fingers.

Total chaos had erupted around them. Women screamed as more blood started to drip from his eyes like tears. Emily felt, rather than heard, as he took his last breath. The plea to keep his small treasure safe etched into the lines of his face.

It was strange, she could hear what was going on all around her but she couldn't seem to process any of it.

"Miss?" A younger man had bent down and was looking at Emily. She tilted her head to look back at him; his face was white. "Are you hurt?" He was talking to her, she knew, but her mind wouldn't register anything he said.

Emily was vaguely aware that Bernadette was not next to her. She was yelling along with hundreds of other voices. Emily felt numb to it all and kept looking at the lifeless stranger in her arms.

****

It was then that Bernadette saw *him*. The giant had returned. He was standing ten or twelve people away; the leer was back on his face. Just like before, the crowd of people seemed to part, moving away from him, and Bernadette saw the long sliver syringe held tightly in one hand.

Understanding dawned, the old man had been poisoned, and whatever was in that vial was very lethal. It only took minutes to work. Bernadette realized that she and Emily had both watched it work!

****

Emily's eyes shot upward to the giant's face. He was glaring at the dead man in her lap. Then his good eye moved to her face and involuntarily her knees turned to jell-o.

His features hardened and he took a step toward her, the syringe disappearing between his long fingers. Emily wasn't able to take a breath for what felt like minutes. Her mind seemed to stop. All she was aware of, all she could think about, was the fact that the giant was getting closer every second.

Then her natural instincts took over. Only one thought possessed her mind, one goal, and the word resounded as it screamed in her head.

RUN!

7

ON THE RUN

Emily felt guilt leaving the dead man's side, but the drive for self-preservation made her feet move.

She flew across the floor, diving in and out of the crowd of people. She dared not look back to see if the giant was behind her. She was sure he was.

Now, as the bustling people thinned out, she could see the exit doors. Rushing toward the doors, she could hear the screaming erupting behind her as more onlookers saw the crumpled, man, lying on the floor.

Emily didn't have time to process what was happening. A hand reached out and grabbed her arm as she flew toward the doors. Her eyes darted to the side. Bernadette was staring at her, questions showing in her eyes that Emily couldn't answer.

****

"Emily?" Bernadette called out as both girls raced toward the rows of parked cars, then crouched behind the nearest one. Emily's face was whiter than Bernadette had ever seen it. She was clutching something in her hands, lips trembling a little, gaze darting.

Emily lifted her face to Bernadette's and something broke behind the green eyes.

"We have to go!" The fear in her voice was evident. "We need to find a way out of here."

"Get in! Now!" Both girls looked up to see Kip three feet from their spot, shoving his passenger door open. Emily seemed to understand the urgent message in his voice and threw herself into the seat of his truck. Bernadette didn't have time to ask questions and followed, dumbfounded.

"Drive." Emily blurted out. "Drive!"

Before Bernadette was even able to pull the door closed, Kip was driving, swerving past cars, heading for the parking lot exit. Bernadette pulled the door shut, working against the force of Kip sailing around the sharp curves. Then more suddenly than she could have thought possible, they were turning left onto a new road. Leaving the airport behind.

****

It was done, he knew. The thorn in his side had been removed. Rainer allowed himself a sip of champagne as a smile of satisfaction spread across his face. He watched the Logan airport buzz with activity from his seat in the back of the black limousine.

Ulric, a giant of a man, had been a good hire on his part. He was a trained killer, mastered in torture and a number of other very unpleasant things. Most likely trained by the American Government, and more deadly than anyone else on the payroll. Rainer liked the man because he didn't ask questions; got in, did what he was paid to do, and got out. He was big to be sure, but he was a ghost and not someone that Rainer would want to cross.

As Rainer enjoyed his victory, some new commotion from the parking lot drew his attention. A dark haired girl, who could have been pretty if it weren't for the sick look on her face, following close behind was a striking red head that was spattered with blood. Both women were running in his direction.

The running girls were keeping low, crouching, then stopped at the back of an old Ford. She seemed to recognize the car and was waiting, eyes scanning in all directions.

Rainer felt a churning in the pit of his belly that made him put down his champagne. Something had gone wrong.

A Forest Ranger pick-up truck suddenly peeled around the cars near the two women and stopped in front of them, blocking his view. When it moved, the girls were gone.

****

Kip glanced at Emily. She seemed to be in a state of shock and was muttering something to herself. It was then that Kip noticed the blood that covered Emily's hands, and spotted her arms and legs.

"She's hurt! We have to get her to a hospital."

"No!" Emily wailed. "No, I'm not hurt, no hospitals, no cops!"

"Emily, what is going on? What happened?" Kip had more questions than she knew what to do with. "I don't understand." Kip took another curve faster than necessary.

"There was this guy… a really big guy." Bernadette was almost stuttering, holding her arms out to brace herself against the dashboard. Kip swung around another curve.

"I saw him, he…the man came barreling through the crowd right at her just after the old man had collapsed. He didn't look like he wanted to *talk*."

"I don't understand. Why would he come after Emily? And what old man? I saw the two of you running in the parking lot and…someone better tell me what is going on!" Kip demanded hitting the steering wheel with his fist.

It was then that Emily seemed to come out of her stupor. She opened her hands and flattened her palms, opening then to reveal a, crumpled, single sheet of folded yellow paper, which was smudged with blood. With it was something silver that Bernadette recognized as a flash drive, a small sleek computer data storage mechanism. But her

66

mind had no time to register what she was looking at because Emily jerked suddenly and threw herself across Bernadette's lap. There was no time to react and she could do nothing but hold her friend as she emptied her stomach onto the floor of Kip's truck.

Emily settled her head into Bernadette's lap. Emily's chest started to tighten with pain. She glanced at Kip. He was rigid, focused, but his eyes met hers for a second and there was something indescribable in them.

"What do we do now?" Bernadette asked.

"I don't know." He said. He slowed the truck and turned off onto another obscure side street. Minutes ticked by with no words spoken between them. Kip kept to side streets and they were soon headed out of town. Emily sat still, watching out the window with eyes that didn't seem to see anything. Somewhere in the distance sirens blared, then faded away. Kip slowed, turned onto a dirt road and stopped.

"We can't go any further until I know what happened." Emily nodded as she sat up and took a deep breath.

8

SUSPECT

Emily finished her story and Bernadette picked up, fitting the pieces together. Kip had let them relate the events without asking questions, absorbing the information, while the three of them took turns cleaning out the cab of his truck. Emily had given the slip of paper and flash drive to Kip. He turned them over and over in his hands. Now she sat, head in her hands, physically and emotionally drained.

"None of us handled this very well." He said looking out toward the city. "I know you were scared, but a man just died and this needs to go to the police."

"He told me not to, and besides, it wasn't what I was thinking about. *Living* was pretty much the only thing on my mind... you didn't see what the giant did to him!" Emily yelled at Kip.

"Running just makes us look guilty! I'm sure after all of this gets cleared up the police won't press charges." He said, talking to himself and rubbing his head.

"What are you talking about?" Emily asked him, her face flushed.

"We left the scene of a crime, and not to put too fine a point on it, but you were the last person to see the old man alive. You ran away and took the only evidence with you." Kip held out his hand to her, the blood stained paper opening on the fold. "Bernadette and I ran with you and now we are implicated as well."

"I never asked for your help!" She screamed up at him.

Bernadette placed a hand on Emily's shoulder and looked at Kip.

"Whatever is going on is not just affecting Emily, it is affecting both of us. This is not your problem, *we* are not your problem." She took the paper and flash drive from him. "You are not part of her... our lives anymore and we would never dream of asking you to be unselfish enough to help anyone. Please just go away, we'll figure this out on our own." Bernadette said with gritted teeth. Kip seemed taken back by her tone.

"I was just saying that..."

"I don't care what you are and aren't saying!" Bernadette burst out, her jaw tight.

"No one asked you to come to our rescue! I wish we'd never ran into you, never seen you." Emily said in a low voice, her head dropping to her chest.

Bernadette slid to her friend's side and put an arm around her. She glared at Kip who looked very lost by Emily's outburst. He took a deep breath and cleared his throat.

"I have a friend on the Billings police force. I could call him and feel out the situation. We are running blind right now and we need to figure out what our next move is." Kip looked into Emily's eyes. "It no longer matters what did or didn't happen, we're in this together now." Emily had the feeling that both of them were discussing a lot more than their flight from the airport. Feeling claustrophobic all three piled out of the cab and drank in the fresh air. Hoping it would clear their minds.

"Call your friend. Let's see if we can find out anything that could help us." Bernadette nodded at him. Kip pulled out his cell phone and dialed a number. They all waited, each holding their breath.

"Yes, hello. I need to talk to detective Smoot. Tell him Kip Morison needs to talk to him." Kip frowned, and then long minutes of silence followed. "Smoot, it's Kip Morison... Yes, it's been a long time. Listen I need to ask you a question. I um, heard something happened at the airport not too long ago. I had some friends there and..." Kip paused as the other man talked, too softly for them to hear.

"A bomb threat? I didn't hear about a... Smoot, look, I have some information about the... Yes, I was flying in... on camera?" Kip was interrupted by the disembodied voice and his eyebrows turned downward in deep thought. Then he lied. "Smoot, I know the man that was killed, he was a friend of mine and I need some answers. I know there was no bomb and I need you to be level with me. I have some information…" Kip hung up the phone then pulled his arm back, and the small cell phone was arched into the air. "We have to move, they were tracking my phone call."

"How do you know?" Emily asked, worry bubbling up in side her.

"Smoot was asking too many pointless questions. He wasn't at all interested in any information and as soon as I mentioned knowing the dead man the conversation became…very strained to say the least, and he knows you two are with me. The long and short of it is that everyone is looking for *you*." Kip looked pointedly at Emily then Bernadette in turn.

"We've got to go back, Emily. The police can protect us." Bernadette pleaded with her friend.

"NO! You didn't see what I saw! No one died in your arms. I saw what that monster is capable of! One second this old man was standing right in front of you and the next he was in my arms, bleeding from his eyes and mouth! It was like his insides were liquefied! I'm not going back!" Her jaw was set in hard lines. "I have to find out what's on this flash drive. They're after whatever information is on it. If I can use it to help keep me safe, to bargain with, I might be able to get out of whatever I just stepped into." Bernadette placed a hand on Emily's shoulder.

"You aren't in this alone." Then both women turned to Kip. He glared at them, both in turn, and then his eyes landed on Emily. The hardness there seemed to soften for a moment, and then he nodded.

"We can't stay here." Kip grumbled and got into the drivers seat of the truck. Emily and Bernadette climbed in the passenger side and took their respective places. "We need to get away from Billings and to a computer."

****

Rainer rubbed his temples with the tips of his fingers. How could two little girls cause him so much trouble? The local police had searched his limousine and he was waved past the barricade set up around the Logan airport. Rainer had left without Ulric; the big man had vanished in the parking lot after the girls had disappeared. There was no need to worry; Ulric would not allow himself to be found.

Rainer was on speakerphone, gathering information to make his next move. After reaching his contacts it had taken no longer than twenty minutes to find out the girl's names, addresses, and even social security numbers. He was sure now that Pinchly had been working alone. The two girls, fleeing the airport, one covered in blood, were no FBI agents, and for that matter, they were no one that Rainer should fear at all. Emily Rivers and Bernadette Brummond were no more than two young girls in the wrong place at the wrong time.

Rainer was confident that his men would be able to find and dispose of the little curly haired hiccup and her sidekick with no more surprises. His only problem at the moment was that she had disappeared into thin air along with her friend and a forest Ranger. Now Rainer seemed to have found himself surrounded by incompetence.

"All I asked for was a list of places the girls may go to ground. In as simple terms as possible, that means, find out all the places our disappearing duo may be running to! I want to know the names of all their teachers, friends, and enemies. You've already failed once with the Ranger." He pounded his fist on the limousine door. "You have ten minutes."

71

"Yes Sir."

"And, Smoot, don't forget, it's not *just* your job that's on the line." The venom in Rainer's voice was unmistakable and his meaning clear.

****

Emily pushed herself away from Kip's shoulder as the truck hit another bump. She struggled to stay in her seat as Kip bounced along yet another dirt road and at the same time was very aware that she was being tossed into him every few minutes. Kip had artfully kept to little known back roads and luckily they had only two cars cross their path. Now on the outskirts of Powell Kip sped up, they all seemed to feel the sense of urgency. There was a feeling of flying blindly into something much lager than themselves.

Kip pulled off the dirt road onto a side street leading into town. Emily could feel all three of them stiffen slightly as cars started to pass by them. It felt like an eternity before Kip pulled off and stopped the truck.

"We'll have to walk from here." Kip said what all of them already knew. The ranger truck would be too easy to spot if they were being tracked. Bernadette and Emily slipped out of the cab and helped Kip remove any personal items. Then he pocketed the keys and grabbed his backpack out of the bed of the truck. Kip set out, Emily and Bernadette close at his heels. Again the trio fell into silence as they traversed the side streets and alleyways of town. With every step they took, Emily felt dread building up. In her gut she knew something was wrong. Then, as their apartment came into view, new fears came to life.

"Stop." She hissed and grabbed Kip's arm. Bernadette had already frozen in place a few paces back, she must have been the first to see the bright red and blue swirling light casting their glow off the white shutters. Kip pulled back and crouched behind a dumpster, Emily and Bernadette followed him.

"What do we do now?" Bernadette whimpered, next to Emily.

"We can't go back to the truck, we can't go home…" Emily bit her lower lip in thought.

"What about Doug's?" Kip breathed. "He doesn't live far. Let's hope no one has made the connection between you and Doug yet." The girls nodded. They were running out of options fast.

"Lets go." Bernadette gathered herself together and, moving low, led the way toward Doug's.

****

Not wanting to be seen entering Doug's small house Bernadette led the others through several back yards until they finally climbed over a low fence and onto Doug's property. Then, without making a sound, she found the hidden key over the door Doug kept for emergencies and unlocked the rarely used back door. Ushering Emily and Kip ahead of her, Bernadette glanced around. The town was quiet. It unnerved Bernadette. She slowly closed the door and turned on her heel, rushing to catch up with the others.

"Doug?" Kip called out into the stillness of the house from the tiny kitchen. There was no answer. "Doug?" He called a little louder this time. A thud came from one of the back rooms then nothing for a moment.

"What? What is going on?" Doug's tall frame appeared in the kitchen doorway. He looked as if he'd been sleeping, clothes disheveled and hair mussed. His eyes fell on Kip in surprise. "Hello." Then they rested on Emily. He smiled a little at her, then his gaze seemed to focus and widened into horror. "Are you hurt? What happened?" Doug's voice seemed to boom in the small space.

"No… none of us are hurt. We have a lot to explain." Bernadette said in a small voice. She had started to shake at the sight of him and collapsed into his arms. Then sobs echoed throughout the house as she crumbled. Doug lowered her to the floor, holding her against him. He looked up into the faces of the only people that could give him answers.

****

Bernadette never left the comfort of Doug's arms as Emily and Kip retold the story that none of them could still quite believe. The emotional strain of the day's events was clearly taking a heavy toll on both girls. Doug moved into the living room and insisted Bernadette lay on the sofa to rest. She closed her eyes and drifted off to sleep. Emily was surprised that she hadn't yet dissolved into a million pieces. She was sure that the only thing keeping her together was some kind of heightened fear, that if her mind started to process her situation, she would lose her mind.

"There's no question about it. We have to contact the police." Doug said in a whisper. Emily was kneeling next to Bernadette, pulling the flash drive and paper out of her hand as she slept.

"If we don't have anything to prove their innocence then Bernadette and Emily could be charged as accessories to murder. Smoot said as much on the phone." Kip growled.

"Not to mention that you helped us to get away." Bernadette said in way of a thank you.

"But they had nothing to do with it!" Doug protested, protectively looking over at his girl friend.

"They have them both on tape. They were standing next to the victim, holding him, and then fleeing the scene." Kip pointed out, his face grim.

"We need to find something that will help us get out of this mess." Emily interjected and tossed the flash drive to Doug. "You're pretty good with computers." He nodded his understanding and left the room. Emily looked from Kip to Bernadette. Her mind was spinning in a million different directions. Doug came back with his laptop and set to work. It was then that Emily remembered the small paper in her hand and unfolded it. *Landry Alston, 1453 Greenwald Ave, Denver Colorado* was written across it in heavy lines.

"He also gave me this." Emily said handing the paper to Doug. "Do you think this Landry Alston could help us?" Doug took the paper and frowned.

"No number. Let's see if we can find out who he is." Doug pulled up his Internet connection and, after a few keystrokes, pulled up a full article on Senator Landry Alston of Colorado. Emily leaned over Doug's chair to read the information. Kip joined them.

"He's the former senator of Colorado. The rest of the article doesn't say anything about him other than his accomplishments in office." Doug started to mutter to himself and typed in a few more searches until he was able to find the last listed phone number for the senator. Emily grabbed a nearby wall phone.

"If we are going to ask for help, now is as good a time as any." She double checked the number and dialed. Out of the corner of her eye she could see Doug working again on a different search.

"Alston Residence, may I help you?" It was a women's voice.

"Yes, I am looking for Senator Landry Alston."

"The Senator is out at the moment. Can I take a message and have him call you back?" Emily hesitated for a moment.

"When do you expect him back?"

"Any moment now, but…"

"I will try back in a few minutes then." Emily said cutting the women off mid-sentence.

"The senator is a busy man, may I please tell him who called or what the call is regarding?" Emily wasn't sure she wanted to tell the women her name and thought fast.

"Yes, this is Professor LaLane from Northwest College in Wyoming. I was wondering if the Senator would have any open dates this fall to attend one of our conferences as a guest speaker? Please have him call me at 307-555-8716, thank you." Emily hung up the phone. She had given a correct number to the woman and hoped that her lie was convincing enough; but, before she could think about it further, Doug broke into her thoughts.

"Look at this!" Kip and Emily both jumped and crowded around him. Doug had been looking up new channels on line and found the story none of them wanted to see. The Billings News channel KTVQ was covering the Logan Airport death as their top story. Doug clicked on the volume and in the left hand corner a dark haired, pretty newswomen came on. She was standing on a strip of grass on the far side of the parking lot behind the yellow tape blocking off the airport.

"...A grizzly murder." They had come in on the middle of her report. "The victim, now identified as Harold Pinchly, lately of Imperial, California, was found dead in the Logan International Airport this morning. He was attacked, eyewitnesses say, by a towering blonde man and possibly two female accomplices. Police have released these sketches of the criminals." A black and white composite drawing of the giant came into view, split screen with a colored still shot of the surveillance cameras in the air port. The image was blurred at best but the bright colored flam tattoo was more than visible.

"Billings police have identified the man and one of the women shown here from a surveillance tape..." In the corner of the screen a video of the airport from earlier that day was playing. Emily could see the giant, Bernadette, and the old man on the screen.

"They are not releasing their names to the public at this time. They have yet to identify the second women and are still looking for any information that may help identify the culprits. If you have any information please call…" The women's voice seemed to trail off as Emily watched in horror at herself, only a few hours before, holding the man in the gray suit as he died in her arms. She never lifted her face to the camera.

Then just as a man's voice came over the speakers asking for any additional information on the deceased man, she saw Bernadette standing next to her, then their dash for the door. Emily closed her eyes not wanting to relive the experience again and took a steadying breath. The pretty dark haired women continued her report.

"The retired investment banker had only recently relocated to San Diego, California, to be closer to his only daughter. While in San Diego, Pinchly had been involved in some part-time consulting for the major trading corporation, Earl Trading Co. Mr. Pinchly's daughter reported him missing four weeks ago when her father never returned home after a day of work.

"When asked by local authorities about her father's disappearance, she reported that her father, in his late sixties, had no signs of early onset Alzheimer's and that it was very unlike him to go any length of time without checking in. Shortly after his disappearance from Earl Trading the CEO reported several million dollars missing.

"There is speculation that Pinchly may have been involved in embezzling the money. We contacted Earl Trading but were told that the company is not ready to make any statements. We'll keep you posted with any new information in this breaking story." Her image faded out and Doug stopped the news clip. He sat back in his chair and ran a hand through his hair.

"Can anything on the flash drive help us?" Emily could hear the hopelessness in her own voice as she talked. Doug seemed to be lost in thought for a moment then bent over his computer. He closed down Windows and brought up other programs in rapid succession. Emily collapsed into a near-by chair and laid her head in her hands. Her brain hurt and thinking rationally was impossible.

She was someplace between insanity and where she now found herself when she could feel Kip's eyes on her. Emily didn't have to look up to see that it was him. The feeling of his gaze on her was electric and something she would not soon forget. Kip took a seat next to her, the only one in the room still empty, and breathed deeply.

"How are you holding up?" The tips of his fingers brushed the top of her knee and stayed there.

"Ok, I guess. Under the circumstances." She muttered, not in the mood to talk. Kip had walked out of her life two months earlier and Emily had come to grips with the fact that she would not see the man again. What hurt worse was that she believed herself to be in love with him. In love; and it took one conversation for him to never look back. If chance hadn't brought them back together then neither would be sitting here having this very conversation. She would not be able to feel the warmth of his hand, to smell his cologne, or hear the smooth tones of his voice.

"Are you hungry? I could get you something." He asked softly. The kindness and concern emanating from his voice made Emily angry.

"No, I don't want anything from you." Her words had more than one meaning and Kip's hand found its way off her knee. Emily didn't feel tired anymore, just irritated and she got up from her chair. "I'm going to…" She didn't finish her sentence, not sure just who she was talking to in the first place and left the room.

"What do you think you're doing?" Bernadette asked angrily.

"Doing?" Kip answered startled that she was awake and glaring at him from the sofa.

"Don't act stupid." She spat and sat upright. "Leave Emily alone!" It was not a suggestion. Kip rose from his chair and looked down at Bernadette, a darkness edging into his face.

"What do you mean? I haven't done anything to her." He matched her anger with his own.

"Do you know what happened to her after you left? Walking away, like she didn't mean anything to you all that time?" Bernadette was almost yelling at him, she was full of fire and not about to back down. "Do you know that she never once had a nightmare after leaving the hospital until the night of the party, and every night after that? Did you know that she would wake up screaming?" Bernadette also stood and inched closer and closer to Kip as she talked. "Don't play dumb with me! When I ask you what your intentions are, try to come up with a better answer, because Emily is my *family* and I will not stand by while you play with her… not again!" Kip raised his hands in a protective movement.

"Wait a minute. I never meant to 'play' anyone." The darkness left his face and his strong features fell just a little. "I never meant to hurt her." He opened his mouth as if he was going to say something more but closed it and looked away.

"She's been through enough. The cave, you, and now this! Keep your distance." Bernadette barked at him, not backing down. Kip seemed stunned and said nothing in response.

Doug still sat in front of the computer, working the keyboard, fingers flying so fast it was astounding. He didn't seem to have noticed any part of the exchange taking place behind him. Bernadette sank back into the sofa. Kip moved to stand near one of the windows, looking out toward the street. The room fell as quiet as a tomb. Emily walked slowly back into the room, and, this time, took a seat next to Bernadette.

Doug stopped typing and squinted at the screen. Everyone's attention turned to him as he sat looking at what seemed to be a blank document.

"What is it?" Kip asked.

"Most of the flash drive is compiled of personal files, like daily journal entries; nothing too spectacular. Then I found this, it's a file buried deep in the memory. Hard to find, I had to search through some junk to find it."

"Are you sure it's not just junk too? I mean, it's blank."

"No Kip, it's not." Doug lifted a hand to signal silence, and then something flashed on the screen and numbers rolled past, one at a time, then in groups. Pages and pages of numbers. Doug leaned forward, back arched in a movement that signaled his confusion.

More typing. Kip leaned over the chair to take a better look at the never ending scrolling numbers. Emily took Bernadette's hand, who had not moved since Doug had taken up working again.

"I almost thought it was just another blank document. But even though it looked blank at first glance I noticed that it seemed to be holding quite a lot of information to not have anything in it. Then I remembered something from when I was a kid. Disappearing ink." No one said anything as Doug talked and worked. "You used to write something, let it dry and watch it disappear. Then the only way to see it was to turn off the light and watch it glow, read it under a black light, or with a special kind of decoder ring, like from the cereal boxes." Doug was rambling now.

"So?" Kip pressed for more information.

"So, we just need to find a way to make the words appear." He stopped typing. "It needs a key." Doug said and sat back in a defeated movement.

"A key?"

"A key word to unlock the code. Whoever put this information on the flash drive did it in numbered code, an encrypted code; a code they made themselves. It needs a key to unlock it. Without the key it would take me forever to decipher the number code." The air hung heavy with the quiet that followed Doug's last statement.

"Judith." Emily whispered.

"What?" Bernadette turned to her friend.

"Judith." Emily said louder this time. "Try Judith."

Doug didn't ask why. He went back to the computer and collectively everyone held their breath. Slowly one letter appeared on the screen amidst the numbers, and then more letters interspersed with the numbers.

"It worked." Kip said amazed and turned to Bernadette and Emily. "How did you know?"

"This is going to take a few minutes." Doug seemed to be oblivious to Emily's unexpected knowledge, or how it affected their situation, as if he had been expecting her to know the answer.

"He told me. The old man at the airport." She breathed, then looked up. "He said *'Keep it safe Judith, at all costs, keep it safe.'* At first I thought it was the ramblings of a dying man, but he was giving me a message." Before anyone could say anything the computer beeped- it was done.

They all rushed to read over Doug's shoulder. After a few minutes lists began to appear, names, and lists of dates. Doug brought up something that caught everyone's attention. Minutes went by as they tried to process what their eyes were seeing.

"Human trafficking." Kip growled, pounding his fist on the table.

9

STOLEN SOULS

The information on the flash drive had been accompanied by photographs. With the evidence in front of them there was no denying what they were seeing. The lists of names, buyers and sellers, the money exchanging hands, the human cattle. It was all there in startling detail; facts, dates, travel routes across the United States. Emily felt her eyes burning and realized she hadn't blinked since starting to read along with the others.

Bernadette was next to Doug as he worked, her eyes darting over pages and pages of names, dates, and files filled with data. She read aloud that most of the girls were sold to sweat shops, working twenty hours a day sewing clothes. They were never let out, threatened and segregated from anyone that could help. Still other's, a very few, were sold to rich households as private servants, nannies and, most often taken out of the country. It wasn't until Bernadette pulled back and turned away that anyone even dared to breathe.

"How could something like this be happening?" Bernadette asked. "How is this possible!"

"I remember hearing something a few years back about some California dress manufacturers paying to have girls come over from Mexico, then stealing their passports, and identification and forcing them to live and work in horrid conditions with no contact to the outside world. I never imagined that anything like *this* was going on in the United States." Doug said, waving a hand toward the computer screen.

Emily felt a tear rolling down her cheek. The compiled information included graphic photos of young girls, their heads shaven, emaciated, some bruised and bloody, being lined up in straight rows. She turned away from the images, eyes misty, and looked out a nearby window.

She felt a chill ripple up her spine; three sleek black cars where pulling up just down the street from Doug's house, tinted windows, and no license plates. Emily shrank back from the window.

"They found us." She squeaked, backing up further and running into a solid mass. Kip grabbed her by the shoulders and moved her behind him. He took a look out the small window and nodded his agreement. Doug and Bernadette said nothing as they worked fast to gather up Doug's laptop off the desk. The flash drive was pocketed as he pushed the computer toward Bernadette. She took it then seemed to turn to stone as Doug pulled at a few cords and shoved them hastily into a black bag. He then reached into one of the desk drawers and started to empty the contents into the bag. Emily felt chills running up her back. She grabbed Bernadette by the arm.

"We have to leave. Now!" She pleaded with her friend. Bernadette seemed frozen to the spot as she watched Doug kneeling to grab paper, brown envelopes, and other seemingly useless things, out of the desk. When he was finished, the bag now slung over one shoulder, he grabbed the closed laptop from Bernadette, and then with his free hand, he cupped her chin.

"Bernadette." His voice as soft as silk.

"I know." Was her simple reply and without any more words being exchanged, the four of them fled the house.

****

Rainer had pulled a few strings, and once again he was one step ahead of the police and found the connection he had been looking for. The girl had a boyfriend, a boyfriend that unfortunately knew a thing or two about computers.

84

The convoy had stopped just down from the boy's house. Rainer didn't really expect to find anyone home but was hoping the small town college kids would have been sloppy enough to leave something behind. His men moved to converge on the small house. Rainer didn't bother to move from his comfortable leather seat as he watched the siege from behind thousand dollar sunglasses.

The shabby looking front door was dispatched off without ceremony and five tall black figures disappeared inside. Not even sixty seconds later his cell phone rang.

"Empty, Sir. Fresh trail out the back. Do we pursue?"

"Clean up the loose ends boys."

****

Doug half pulled, half carried Bernadette down the ally. They were out of eyesight of his house but he still felt the need to move faster. Bernadette felt like her feet were made of lead as she crept along next to Doug. The sounds around her were amplified by the fear driven adrenaline pumping in her veins. Ahead of them she heard the grip of tires on asphalt. They slowed, then stopped, but the engine idled.

Being cautious, Kip, Emily and Doug all scurried behind a tall wood fence to stay out of sight. Bernadette left Doug's side and against the hissing protests of her friends, peeked around the corner.

A Jeep had stopped two houses down the block from them. A short man jumped out, leaving the Jeep running, walked toward the front door of a house. Bernadette made her move before the stout stranger had even rung the doorbell. She sprinted toward the Jeep, flinging herself at the driver's side door.

"Let me." Kip said grabbing her shoulder. He hurriedly helped her into the back seat and pushed his long frame behind the steering wheel.

"No, we are not stealing someone's car." Emily protested as Doug jumped into the Jeep alongside Bernadette.

"Do you have any other suggestions?" Kip retorted. "Get in Emily." His tone was sharp and made Emily feel like she was being scolded like a child. Yet, she slid into the passenger side and flung her door closed as he pulled away from the curb.

10

HIGHER GROUND

Emily clung to the Jeep door, holding herself as far away from Kip as humanly possible in the small space. She stared out the window as they drove on obscure dirt roads from town to town. Doug and Bernadette whispered in the back seat to each other, minds working on a way out of the mess they found themselves in. Emily wanted to pay attention, to contribute, yet, she stayed silent.

Kip left the dirt road, turning toward a set of purple-blue mountains Emily recognized. They only have one other small town to drive through before they would reach the base of the Big Horns. It had been suggested that they spend the night in Kip's ranger's cabin. But the idea was overruled in favor of a more out of the way place, a cabin that would not be directly linked to Kip unless someone did some serious digging. Emily knew it was a better idea than playing the part of sitting ducks at the ranger's cabin but she was annoyed that their destination was Kip's ex-girlfriend's summer home. Apparently she would not be there due to the July holidays, and for that reason alone, Emily was grateful.

It would buy them a little time to try and reach Senator Landry Alston and pray he would be able to help them; but to keep that thought a priority was hard when her mind kept going back to Kip with someone else, even an ex-someone. It made her feel uneasy.

Kip slowed down as they reached the outskirts of town. Emily kept her eyes on the passing scenery. People milled around shops and teenagers jay-walked down the street. Lovell, Wyoming. She had spent too much time in this little town to suit her taste and it brought back bitter sweet memories. As the Jeep crawled past more of the downtown area, something out of place caught her eye.

A lean, dark haired man was standing near one of the street corners next to a bank. He was dressed from head to toe in one of the finest tailored suits she had ever seen outside of a wedding. His black tresses gleamed in the sunlight. For the middle of summer, the hottest time of the year, he looked oddly out of place. But it wasn't just his looks that caught Emily's eye. It was the way he sneered as his gaze caught sight of their Jeep. For a split second, as they drove past, his icy blue eyes caught hers and held. It sent a shiver up her spine. Then the Jeep pulled past the bank and the man was out of sight.

****

Rainer stood on the edge of the sidewalk; bank on one side of him, a church on the other. This was going to be easier than he thought.

The stolen Jeep had been easy to spot and track. But as they headed out of town Rainer fell back. They hadn't gone to the police, how much could they really know? But he was under orders and could take no chances. It would be better to gain the upper hand with surprise. The further away from civilization he let them get, the simpler dispatching of the troublesome little group would be.

Smoothing back his already immaculate hair, Rainer walked a few steps and surveyed his surroundings. Where to start?

Down the block to the right he saw a small local pizza parlor. Close to the pizza parlor was a sign for a diner. He decided on the diner, a pizza parlor would be full of children and Rainer detested children. The diner would do just fine.

Walking through the door he could see he had made the right choice. The place was small and empty with, some of what could be considered, local charm. Rainer

88

considered none of it; he saw none of it, his well-trained mind was on his one and only task.

"Hello." A short, round, unattractive women smiled at him from behind the counter. *"Yes, this would be easy."*

"Good afternoon." He said pleasantly and flashed a winning smile.

"Can I get you anything?" She asked clearly dazzled by the pale, handsome, well dressed stranger.

"A cup of coffee would be nice, thank you." He sat on a barstool. She poured him a cup and placed it lightly in front of him. She was still smiling, unable to keep her eyes off him.

Rainer smiled too, bigger this time, but for a very different reason. He was a talented man and his talents enabled him to extract information, information that was sold to the highest bidder. But, this time, all information would be handed to him on a silver platter, with little effort and no trouble. He loved small towns, everyone was so trusting.

It took less than a minute to find out the Ranger's name. A few more minutes of intense gazing and flattery he walked out of the diner, address in hand.

A slick black cell phone flipped open and he breathed into it. "I have them."

****

Bernadette's eyes felt like they were on fire. She knew she should give in and try to rest but her mind wouldn't stop racing. Doug sat next to her in the cramped back seat of their stolen Jeep, his long fingers wrapped around hers. She was glad he wasn't asking her all kinds of questions she didn't have answers for.

Kip rounded another corner in the road and Bernadette slid toward Doug. She allowed herself to fall into his side. Doug let go of her hand and reached his arm around her shoulders and kept her firmly next to him. Bernadette relaxed a bit next to his warmth then tried desperately not to close her eyes, afraid that to see the old man's chalky face in her minds eye. So, she concentrated on other things, like what her mother would have done when Bernadette hadn't gotten off the plane in Las Vegas. She felt a pang of sadness at the thought.

Bernadette felt her head lulling a bit. Maybe it wouldn't be so bad to rest a little. Letting her eyes close she leaned closer to Doug, in turn he pressed his lips to the top of her head and let them linger, his breath in her hair.

"Bernadette." Doug's voice was so far away. Bernadette could still feel his arms around her, smell his cologne, feel the gentle rustle of his hair. But something else was lurking all around her. A darkness she couldn't seem to escape from. "Bernadette." He called her name again and Bernadette woke with a start.

"It's okay baby, we're at the cabin." Doug breathed the words next to her ear. "It's okay." He said again. It was then Bernadette realized she had fallen asleep and must have been having some kind of nightmare. Her cheeks felt hot and wet. Reaching up she brushed tears from her eyes.

Doug took her face in his hands, turning it upward, forcing her to look at him. He dried her tears with soft fingers. Bernadette felt the darkness of her dream fading. He smiled at her, his eyes warm with affection. She tried to smile back.

"Everything will be fine. I promise." He said, and before she could respond he kissed her. Bernadette held him, returning the kiss, a sweet painful kiss. She wished that Doug were right, needing to believe he was. It was all she had.

****

Emily jumped out of the Jeep as soon as the engine had been turned off. The display of emotion in the back seat was more than she could handle at the moment. Instead she walked away from the scene, arms wrapped around herself, and gazed up at the brilliant blue canvas, the deep hues of rich green in the trees and the cobalt mountains.

Behind her stood a small log cabin set back off a twisting dirt road. The setting was impressive to say the least and would have inspired awe from almost anyone. It was picturesque and charming and Emily hated everything about it. The bitterness she felt came from the cabin's owner and not the perfect setting. *"Kip's ex-girlfriend."* Emily thought the words angrily.

"Pretty, isn't it?" His voice startled Emily. She didn't turn to look at him.

"I was just thinking how unremarkable it looked to tell the truth." Emily thought to herself but didn't say anything out loud.

"Come inside, I'll get you something to eat." It was a strange thing to say at the moment Emily thought.

"Something to eat?" She asked.

"It's late afternoon." He offered as an answer.

"And?"

Emily turned to face Kip. "And, I thought you might like something."

"Stop it, would you!" She snapped. "Stop being nice to me. All it does is throw me off. I've gotten used to the surly, rude, arrogant, Kip. I don't know what to do with *this* one." She said, pointing her hand at him to emphasize her words. Emily instantly regretted opening her mouth because she got just what she asked for and not what she really wanted. Kip's eyes were dark again, his face expressionless. He nodded, turned and walked toward the cabin. Emily hung her head. She felt silly, young, stupid, and all the things that must have pushed him away in the first place.

Bernadette and Doug had climbed their way out of the Jeep, both stood looking from Emily to Kip. She turned her back on them and looked at the sky again, wishing its endlessness would swallow her.

"Come on." Emily heard Doug say to Bernadette. "Give her some time alone." Emily shook her head. She didn't want time alone. She wanted all of this to go away, to turn back time to this morning and change things! She didn't want to be stuck in some cabin in the mountains with Kip, she didn't want to be running, and she didn't want to know what she knew. The weight of all of it was crushing down on her. How would they ever get out from under what had happened in the last twelve hours?

Emily squared her shoulders and walked to the cabin. The door was open and Kip had disappeared inside. The three of them followed. It took some adjusting to the dim light to tell what she was seeing.

They had stepped into one large room. A stone fireplace dominated the far wall, flanked by two picture windows and fat, hand carved bookcases. The large room served as kitchen, living area and bedroom.

"Through there is the bathroom." Kip muttered pointing at the only other door in the room. "There is running water if you want to clean up." He said, nodding toward Emily and Bernadette. "I'll get the lights turned on."

"Thank you." Bernadette said when Emily didn't respond, and disappeared behind the door.

Kip walked to the far side of the room and flipped open the breaker box. Soon bulbs blazed, lighting the cabin. It was just as charming inside as it had been out. There was an old leather couch that looked comfortable and inviting, wooden end tables and a coffee table that matched the hand carved look of the bookcases.

The sleeping area consisted of a large brass bed that sat in one corner next to a single dresser. The kitchen took up the space just off the main entrance. Lining the wall stood an antique refrigerator, stove, sink and cabinets. A small breakfast nook nestled next to the large picture window. Checkered red and white gingham curtains were hanging over it.

Emily took it all in, the woolen blankets, woven rugs, patchwork quilt, picturesque wrought-iron lamps with stained glass shades, large wildlife paintings. The little details in the room brought all the elements together. Yet, what caught her eye, was a tall-backed chair off to one side of the couch. The carved detail and size of the chair was astounding. It sat atop, what she assumed must be a bear skin rug.

"Beautiful." She breathed from her spot in the doorway. Kip turned and for a moment their eyes met. Emily thought she saw the hard lines on his face soften and something indescribable burning in his dark eyes. Her lungs seemed to catch and it was more than the thin mountain air that was making it hard for her to breath. She felt herself being drawn into his gaze. Then just as quickly as the skip of her heartbeat, it was gone. Hard darkness glimmered in his gaze and he turned away from her.

Doug hadn't noticed the exchange and went about setting up his computer on the table, grabbing items from his bag and spreading them out in front of him.

"You'll find a plug off to the right." Kip offered as Doug pulled cords out of the bag and started to hook them up. Emily walked in far enough to allow the front door to close. Kip walked into the small kitchen area and started to pull cans from the cupboards.

"Let me," Emily whispered as an apology. She stepped next to him.

"Fine." He growled but didn't move from his spot. Emily took the can of beans from his hand and set to work. For what felt like hours Kip stood off to one side watching her. Then he left his post and went to the dresser near the bed. This time Emily found herself watching him. He opened a few different drawers until he found what he must have been looking for. Pulling out a shirt and pair of jeans he turned back to face Emily. She now had a big pot of pork and beans cooking on the stovetop and a small pan of corn bread in the oven.

"I was thinking that maybe you'd like something clean." He said handing the clothes to Emily.

"Thank you." She said, taking them from him, their fingers brushing. Emily walked over to the bathroom door and tapped lightly.

"Bern?" There was no answer. Emily tried the door handle, turning it slowly. "I'm coming in." She announced and pushed back the door. Bernadette sat on the floor, knees pulled up underneath her chin, rocking back and forth. Emily rushed in, shutting the door behind her.

"Oh Bernadette!" Kneeling down next to her friend she placed an arm around her shoulders.

"How do we fix this?" Bernadette asked behind a curtain of tears.

"I don't know. I can't stop from seeing his face and now it's just gotten worse. I see their faces too, those young girls in the pictures." Emily felt the tears she had been holding back burning the backs of her eye lids and spilling freely down her face.

"This is too big for us to deal with alone." Bernadette sobbed.

"Your right Bern, this is too big for just the four of us. But what if it wasn't just the four of us?"

"What are you talking about?" Bernadette asked in confusion.

"Let me get cleaned up and change. Then I'll come out and explain." Emily said brushing the last of the tears from her face.

****

By the time Emily had come out of the bathroom, dusk had fallen heavily over the mountains. She could never remember the sky being so big before and, despite herself, she marveled at the rich canvas of colors that kissed the mountains as the sun made its final descent behind their towering peaks. She hurried to make dinner.

"Okay everyone, come get a plate and then I have something I want to discuss." Emily said as she dished up plates, placing them on the kitchen counter. Bernadette gladly took hers and sank into the leather couch. The warm corn bread was heaven and she couldn't remember a time that beans had ever tasted better. All of them ate until the food was gone.

"You said you have something to tell us." Kip said from the high-backed chair, leaning forward to place his now empty plate on the coffee table.

"Yes... Yes, I think I have an idea on how to help us get out of this mess, kind of."

"Okay, shoot." He said folding his arms across his chest.

"Well, I was just thinking about our reaction to seeing those photos and reading parts of the files and it occurred to me that, well, anyone who saw them would feel the same way. So I was wondering if you," Emily said looking at Doug, who had spent his time since reaching the cabin setting up all the equipment he had managed to bring with him. "Could you make some copies, something we could get into the hands of the media? We know we can't go to the cops. Bernadette, Kip and I will all be arrested and that information swept under the rug. This is bigger than any of us, but if we can get this into the hands of the public..."

"That's not a half bad idea." Doug said scratching his chin. "It will take a while to decode all the files and see what is the most important but I think it might just work."

"It's a great idea!" Kip said unfolding his arms. "If the American public at large knew about this, the government would have to take action. People wouldn't rest until something was done about it. It would also give us a chance to try and prove our innocence in the death of that man."

"*Our* innocence?" Emily asked. "It wasn't your face on the news today!"

"No, your right, it wasn't. But regardless, we are all in this together now and I'm sorry I ever implied anything otherwise." Both Bernadette and Emily looked hard at Kip. His face was sincere.

"You're right. The national outcry would be too great for anyone to ignore." Bernadette said with excitement and hope in her voice.

"So, all we have to do is get this information into the Public eye via the Media and, until then, lay low from whoever wants their flash drive back." Doug said more to himself than to anyone else. He looked up into the faces of those around him. "Let's get to work."

****

Emily curled her legs tighter underneath herself as she lay next to a sleeping Bernadette on the big iron bed. Doug was still seated in front of his computer, it's screen the only light in the room. After deciding what to do next, he had set to work sifting through files. Emily had to admit to herself that Doug had shown a presence of mind none of the others had when he had thought about grabbing items out of his desk.

Emily rolled over; listening to the bed moan under her movements. Her eyes landed on Kip's sleeping form and she instantly regretted moving. He sat in the large chair, legs stretched out in front of him, hat tipped over his eyes, arms folded across his chest. The scene was a disturbing formula and Emily was thrown backward in time to a very different night. She sighed at the memory and once again shifted her weight. Now lying on her back, eyes glued to the ceiling, she allowed herself to truly not think about anything, willing her mind to go blank and her limbs to relax.

Scared to close her eyes because a ghostly face kept staring back at her with unblinking eyes. She had seen someone die, not just pass away in their sleep, but with violent shutters.

What kind of people were after them? If one injection could dissolve a man into a mass of blood within a matter of minutes, what would happen to them if captured? The idea sent a cold shiver down her spine.

It seemed as if only seconds had ticked by as she lay there, but now it wasn't a soft bed under her, it was the jagged cold rocks of the cave. Emily shivered and bit back a terrified scream. Willing her eyes to open but meeting only blackness, she waited, but this time no one was coming for her and she knew it. This time the unanswering darkness would envelop her and keep it's secrets.

****

Thursday July 17th

"Emily, get up." Bernadette took her friend by the shoulders and shook her hard. Emily was having another nightmare and Bernadette wanted her to snap out of it before Kip came back into the cabin. "Emily, everything is alright." She said, softer this time. The pale face yielded nothing but there was a flutter of her eyes.

"Bern?" Her voice was weak.

"Yes, it's me. Open your eyes." The lids flew open and green questioning eyes met Bernadette's brown ones. "You were having a nightmare." She said as an answer to the unspoken question.

"Sorry." Emily looked around the room.

97

"The boys are gone, for the moment." Bernadette helped Emily to her feet. "Was it the cave again?"

"Yes, and you know, after yesterday I thought I would have dreamed about the airport, but it's the feeling of being lost I can't seem to shake." Emily shivered a little.

Bernadette shook her head.

"I didn't dream at all. It kind of bothers me. I felt like I should have, like I should be in some kind of shock. Maybe it hasn't hit me yet. Or maybe it's because right now my reality is worse than my dreams ever could be?" Emily placed a hand on Bernadette's shoulder as they slumped forward. The rest of the conversation was cut short as the front door banged open.

"They're here!" Doug stormed into the room. He was out of breath and he looked strained. Bernadette jumped off the edge of the bed.

"What?"

"Kip and I walked over to where he has his cabin, right? There are three black cars parked all around it and two more just down the road. They're the same ones we saw at my house, I'm sure of it!" Doug, who was always clam and collected, was wild, with something close to fear edging into his voice.

"Where is Kip?" Emily asked.

"What do we do?" Bernadette followed with her own question.

"We're pretty sure that no one saw us and this cabin is far enough away from Kip's that we should be safe for a while, or at least I hope we are." Doug was talking to Bernadette, ignoring Emily. "I ran back to make sure that neither of you had left the cabin. Kip stayed to see if he could gather any more information. We've got to hurry!" Doug ran a hand through his hair and tried to steady his breathing. He sat down in front of his computer and flipped it open.

"We can't just sit here all day. What do we do?" Bernadette asked again, forcing Doug to look at her.

"We have to get the files I've been able to open burned onto these CD's and get them ready to send in the mail. Then, I don't know- we'll have to find someplace else to hide until...until..."

"Until when? We have no idea how long it's going to take for someone to look at one of the CD's or for the story to break! By now these guys aren't the only ones looking for us. How long until someone finds the connection between Kip and whoever owns this cabin? How long do we really have with these *people* already on the mountain?" Bernadette was yelling, her eyes crazed, hands flying as she talked. Doug got back to his feet and grabbed her by the arms, forcing her to look at him.

"Stop it!" He barked at her. "What other choice do we have? We can't just waltz into the local police station anymore. We're way past that!" He took a few deep breaths and gathered Bernadette into a fierce hug. Emily looked away, color rising to her face.

"I'll do everything I can, Bernadette. You just have to trust me. We'll have to trust each other. It's all we have left." The tenderness in his voice brought tears to Bernadette's eyes. She clung to him, wanting badly to believe that things would turn out, but doubt was stronger than hope as they played tug of war with her emotions.

"He's dead." The front door had once again flung open and Kip's large frame was silhouetted in it.

"Who?" Asked Doug not relenting his hold on Bernadette.

"Senator Alston." Kip was somber as he shut the door behind him. "On my way back I stopped at the Jeep to see if I could catch the latest on the news. It seems that the

Senator was found dead, along with his family, in their home…" Kip looked down. "Shot in the head from behind, execution style."

Emily rose from the bed, "His whole family?"

"Even his two grandchildren." Kip confirmed. "It seems someone is trying to send us a message." The room fell into silence for a long time as each of them tried to process this new information.

"Then let's send them a message of our own!" Doug said, a hard look flashing across his face.

11

CONSEQUENCE

Emily felt stunned. Had it only been yesterday that she had talked to someone at the Alston household? Could they have led the killers right to their door and not have known? The thought sent shivers down her back; only yesterday things had been so normal. Had it really only been yesterday that Doug had come by to see Bernadette off to her family reunion? Yesterday that they had slept in? Yesterday that a man had been killed in front of them? It seemed impossible, yet, now she found herself sitting on one of the hard wooden chairs, feeling like she was living a dream as Doug burned the CD's Bernadette stared blindlessly into space and Kip poured over a map.

"You'll have to take the girls and take the Shell Highway to Greybull." He was saying to Doug. "They'll be watching the Highway 14A to Lovell, but you should be able to get into town without anyone noticing the Jeep. Once you have mailed the disks you'll have to wipe down the Jeep and dump it. I'll try to lead them in the wrong direction for as long as I can." Emily stopped listening. She felt numb all of the sudden and the air in the cabin seemed to choke her. The heat was stifling, suffocating, and she had to get out.

"I need to step outside for a minute." She muttered and walked out the door. The warm sunshine felt good on her face. She didn't go far but sat down in the still damp grass near the cabin and looked into the clear sky. The peace all around her seemed to be in such contrast with her life at this moment.

"What is a pretty little thing like you doing out here all alone?" Emily gasped and jumped to her feet. A tall blonde man smiled at her. He was dressed from head to toe in camouflage, and it didn't escape her notice that he had a rifle slung over one shoulder.

"I…I." She stammered.

"Honey! I have been looking all over for you!" Kip was standing next to her so fast that she wasn't even sure how he had gotten there.

"I just wanted some fresh air." Emily tried to smile as Kip put an arm around her. He was putting a hand out in greeting toward the blonde.

"Hi, Carl Write. This is my wife Lacey." The blonde man took Kip's hand and the two men exchanged a friendly handshake.

"Quill. I was just passing by, on a hunting trip." He said pointing to the gun. "Must have lost my bearings and got turned around a bit. I saw the cabin from the road and then saw your wife. Thought I would stop and ask for directions." His eyes still held Emily in their gaze, making her feel uncomfortable with the attention.

"I'll be happy to help. Where are you headed?" Kip was smiling, but Emily could tell he was tense, his hand gripping her side tightly. Quill didn't have time to answer, a loud voice boomed over the radio pinned to his hip.

"Quill, report." He grabbed at the sleek black box.

"Quill here."

"Where are you?" The voice was low, nothing more than a rumble of sound. Then nodding to Kip and Emily, he turned away from them, walking far enough away that they could only catch a few of the words being spoken.

"Get inside!" Kip hissed between clenched teeth. Emily turned on her heel and half walked, half ran inside.

Neither Doug or Bernadette said a word to her, all three of them looked out different windows at Kip and the stranger. They seemed to be exchanging words for a few minutes and then the man named Quill turned, gave Kip a friendly nod of the head, and left. Kip didn't return to the cabin until Quill was well out of sight. When he did start to walk back the look on his face was more than enough to scare Emily. She edged to the opposite side of the room as the door burst open.

"How much more time do you need?" He asked Doug.

"I'm not positive. Hours maybe."

"You can't stay here. Gather all your things, you and Bernadette are leaving."

"Leaving? Where will we go?" Bernadette took a small step closer to Doug. Kip grabbed a backpack and was rummaging around the kitchen, grabbing items out of drawers and tossing them into the bag.

"You'll take the Jeep, use only the roads I tell you," He said, pen in hand, bending over the map he had looked over with Doug the night before, outlining a new path. "You'll pass some larger family summer homes but I want you to go farther up…" Kip and Doug bent over the map.

Emily felt helpless. They had to run again and now Kip was separating from them, trying to keep them safe by acting as a decoy.

"You'll find a small place, owned by a cattle rancher, you should be able to hide there until the disks are done. We'll try to double back and meet you but if…" Kip paused. "Then follow the same path we talked about before down the mountain."

"Bernadette, help me pack this up." Doug said pulling on cords. She rushed to his side. Kip then turned to Emily. She felt the breath in her lungs turn cold at the look in his eyes.

He didn't say a word to her, and that was worse than if he had yelled. She felt her stomach churning. Emily knew she had made a mistake.

"What about you?" Bernadette asked, ending the quiet that was holding the room in its grip.

"My *wife* and I will be setting up camp up the road. Quill may only be muscle but whoever is looking for us is not going to let us walk away again. If they knew about Doug so soon after the incident at the airport, you can bet they know what the rest of us look like."

Bernadette seemed to think about what Kip had said for a minute, then jumped. "*Your wife?*" She questioned.

Kip had turned back to Emily.

"I'm sorry." She managed to force out. Kip had walked over to where she stood holding onto the wall for support. He was so close now she could feel the soft current of his breath in the still air around her.

"I don't need you to be sorry Emily, I need you not to be so stupid!"

12

PURSUIT

Doug had been bent over the laptop for what seemed like hours. Bernadette, who stopped walking back and forth across the cabin floor, was now settled in a seat near the front window. Her breath was fogging the glass, but she couldn't take her eyes off the road that stretched out in front of her, the dipping down behind the rolling hills of their new hiding place. Bernadette only wished that Emily and Kip would return soon so that they could plan their next move. They had been gone all day and dusk was setting in.

As Bernadette sat near the large cabin window, head in her hands, eyes staring out into the dimming light of day, her mind raced with possible answers as to what was keeping them.

Doug sat facing his laptop, waiting for the files to be copied. Both said nothing. The stillness in the air was becoming deafening to Bernadette so she rose to her feet and walked the floor. Doug pushed back from his chair and came to her side.

"She's fine. Kip will keep her safe. I'm sure they're not close enough to use their walkie-talkies or…"

"Or what?" She snapped. "Or someone has found them, or she is dead." Doug grabbed Bernadette by the shoulders.

"No one is going to die! We'll find a way out of this." He pulled her toward him, holding her gently in his arms.

"We should never have separated. If anyone gets hurt… I should have never…never…" A shiver rippled up her back. "When I close my eyes I still see his face in my mind, an unreal chalky whiteness, laying in Emily's arms." Doug pressed his lips to the top of her head.

"We're doing the right thing. Right now it's the only thing we can do." He said softly. Bernadette closed her eyes.

"We are doing the right thing." She allowed herself a moment to enjoy being held in his arms and put hers around him. "I just hope Emily and Kip are alright."

****

Emily felt like her feet were going to be nothing more than bloody stumps at the end of her legs. She had been following Kip for hours. The sun, high in the sky, now started to dip down, but Kip never slowed down. She didn't ask him where they were going, what his plan was or if they would ever stop. She couldn't stand seeing brush after brush on trails so thin they could almost be nonexistent. The heat of the sun was burning her skin. Without looking at her, Kip reached into his backpack and pulled out a canteen of water and took a drink. He handed her the canteen and slowed his pace for the first time in hours. Leaning on a nearby tree, she gladly took the water and chance for a rest.

"Stay. I'm going up over that ridge and make sure Quill is still following us." Kip said and turned to leave.

"Quill?" She asked, gulping more water.

"Yes, your new boy friend, and a few of his friends have been on our tail from the time we left." Emily was surprised, she had no idea they were being followed.

"We've been leading them away from Bernadette and Doug." She said to herself.

"These guys are too organized not to know what Bernadette's closest friend looks like." He eyed her with something like disgust. Emily could tell he was still angry at how she had put all of them in danger by going out into the open, by letting herself be seen.

Kip didn't say anything else, took the canteen from her hands and left her by the tree and walked away at a brisk pace.

Emily sat and turned her eyes toward the sky. It was a deep blue, bright and cloudless. Her feet throbbed and felt swollen inside her shoes. She felt sick, hot, sweaty and too tired to close her eyes. The mountains were quiet, it was unnerving. Emily took another long drink of water and squinted into the distance. Something reflected in the sun in the distance and shot a blinding light in her direction. Emily shielded her eyes.

"Did you really think I wouldn't recognize you?" She could feel his breath on her neck and didn't have to look to know it was *him*. Quill, was standing behind her. "You and your friend, Miss Brummond, were kind enough to supply photos and personal information on all your closest acquaintances." His lips brushed the nap of her neck. "But no photo could do you justice." Quill was laughing at her and held up a photo of Emily and Bernadette that used to hang on their refrigerator back home.

Emily felt her heart beating wildly in her chest. Where was Kip and what was she going to do? In the distance the bright spot that had been blinding her while Quill crept up behind her had materialized into four other men dressed in camouflage from head to toe. All were tall, well muscled and menacing.

"It's time." He said now standing at her side.

"Time?" Emily choked.

"The flash-drive please." Quill put out his hand to her just as they were met by his men.

"I… I don't have it." She gulped.

"We'll see." He nodded to one of the men and Emily was lifted to her feet. Quill was still uncomfortably close to her. He reached over and brushed the hair out of her face, smiling. "Search her." Emily was roughly handled as hands grabbed at her; patting her down for something she didn't possess.

"She's clean." The man said and stepped back into line with the others.

"So, your *husband* has it, does he?" Quill asked. "Well then we'll just have to make him come to us." He grabbed Emily by the arm and pulled her after him.

"No." She managed to gasp, looking around for any sign of Kip.

****

"Quill, report." Rainer barked into his radio.

"I have the red haired girl, she doesn't have anything on her." Quill's voice answered.

"What about the others?" Rainer was angry. The mercenaries he had working under him didn't seem to feel the same irritation about this pebble in his shoe. "This is taking too long, they are just a bunch of college kids!"

"I have men following the other two. We'll have them soon enough."

"You'd better." Rainer slammed down the radio and took a long drag from his cigar. Once his nerves had settled a bit he sat back in his seat, the air conditioning blasting though the limo.

It had been six days; six days racing around the midwest after an elderly man, and now four nobodies. Rainer had never allowed such sloppy work from his men before. He had never had to search so long for anyone. His skills had taken him to many locations around the world. He had been employed by some of the richest and most powerful people in the world to clean up their indiscretions.

Rainer glanced out the window at the passing trees and seethed. He hated nature. But then again it was fitting, in a way, to have such abundance and opportunity around him to dispose of the bodies without them ever being discovered.

"Ulric, if Quill is unsuccessful you may have to clean up the lose ends yourself. I can't let this drag on any longer. The men we work for are getting impatient for results." Ulric fixed his good eye on Rainer and nodded his understanding.

****

The walls were closing in; Bernadette could feel the stale air in the dusty cabin crushing down on her. Doug was still decoding files. Bernadette tried to concentrate on something else and glanced around the cabin. This one was a little larger than the one they had spent the night in. But poorly furnished, other than the fact it had power and running water you wouldn't have been able to tell it was ever in use. Layers of dust covered every inch of the empty shelves, counter tops, small wooden chairs and table.

Neither had said anything for hours. Bernadette knew she was weak with hunger and too tired to even close her eyes. Images flashed in her mind, the airport, the black cars, a giant man towering over the crowd, and a former senator and his family murdered.

"It's not going to work." She said before the words registered in her mind.

"What?" Doug asked looking up, his eyes strained and red.

"What were we thinking?" Bernadette blurted out. "We can't do this! We can't pray that someone, anyone will help us even after the information gets out. We can't hide in these mountains forever! We can't! We...we..." She was sobbing now; knees giving out she sank to the floor in despair. Doug was by her side in an instant placing his arms around her.

"Bern, it's okay." He whispered into her ear, rustling her dark curls. "Something will happen and everything will work out." *Doug was right*, she thought. Something was going to happen, she could feel it in the air, it almost crackled with life around her, something was happening and she was powerless to stop it. The tears stopped. She felt the salt of them dry on her face.

****

Emily licked her lips; it had been hours since her captures had allowed her to stop walking or take a drink. She could tell by the clear path the sun had taken across the sky, it would be late afternoon by now. She felt weak and a deep kind of illness that she couldn't explain. Quill and the other men had not used the radio in a while and had kept off the main mountain trails. She had no way of knowing where they would take her, only that she had to come up with a way out before they reached their destination.

Quill stepped out of his position in the lead and stepped next to Emily. "This would be a lot easier on you if you would just give us what we came for." He said taking a long drink from his canteen; water glistened at the corners of his mouth. Emily didn't say a word. "I guess it really won't matter. *Your* better half will be along soon to try and collect you I'm sure." Quill's lip turned upward into a sneer. "He'll try, at least." The way his eyes rested on her face made Emily want to shiver.

She rubbed at the rope binding her hands together as sweat dripped down her arm and burned the raw skin underneath. Quill smiled at her with a kind of satisfied power.

"Only precaution." He said pulling on the ties. "Not that you have any place to run." He said still very satisfied with himself. Emily kept her eyes forward; trying to hide the panic feeling that was rising in her. He was right, where would she run to? But would being lost in the mountains and dying of exposure be any better than the fate she now faced?

"Quill, it's him," one of the large men said handing Quill a crackling radio.

"Quill here."

"How close are you to the rendezvous?" Quill winked at Emily and walked a distance away from her. Another one of his men met him with a topographical map. They had stopped their progress for a minute and Emily sank into the tall grass. She felt

110

her weary bones crying out for the rest but something sharp was biting into her leg. Emily moved her leg just a little and felt hope rush over her. She gathered the glittering stone into her hand and pushed it up into the ropes holding her hands together.

Emily strained to hear anything of the conversation going on between Quill and whoever was waiting for them. Praying her actions had not been noticed by Quill or any of the other men.

"Yes Sir." Quill looked at his watch and then up at the sky. "Before dark. No problem." Emily felt like the sound of her own breath, labored and heavy was loud in her ears; too loud to hear what else was being said. Then Quill was back by her side, his boots crushing the undergrowth at her knee.

"Time to go, Girly." He barked and pulled her up by the shoulder.

"Please." Emily breathed. "Water." It was all she could say. Quill looked at her for a moment, thinking over the request. He pulled out his canteen. Emily felt a surge of gratitude; he was going to let her drink. But just as the glimmer of hope appeared, it died. Quill uncapped the top of the canteen and poured the contents onto the ground at Emily's feet, smiling as he did so.

"Quill, what if she faints? She looks pretty bad." It was the large man with the map that addressed Quill.

"She doesn't look that bad." Quill pulled Emily close to his side, one arm around her waist, the other under her chin to tilt her face upward. "I'll take care of her if she faints, don't you worry about that." Emily felt her head swim as the stench of his breath hit her face. He laughed and pushed her forward. "Lets go."

Emily stumbled a little then found her footing and moved forward. Her brain was on fire, trying to find a way out. Even if she was able to cut the ropes with out bringing attention to herself she still had to get away. As the sun continued to dip further down in the sky she felt the last of her strength leaving her body. Then as she was tugged along the sharp rock cut into her wrist renewing her.

****

Rainer slipped the sunglasses back on and turned his face away from the glaring sun. The stench of pine trees filled his nostrils and made him want to vomit. Nature. Just one of the many on along list of things in this world that he loathed. He glanced down at his feet, the toes of his shiny black, leather loafers, floating off the precipice of a cliff. He smiled, a wicked smile and spat over the vast space underneath him.

The wind kicked up and swept around him. It gave him the feeling of falling, flying, and, most of all, power. The radio crackled, alive, and fussed.

"Sir. We may have a problem." Quill's voice came over the receiver. Rainer felt annoyance toward the man welling up inside him. He had used Quill on other jobs. He was good, well as long as he was paid. But Quill was sloppy and had the tendency to let a pretty face cloud his actions.

"What is it?" Rainer barked, stepping back from the ledge. There was a long, uncomfortable silence as he waited.

"She...the girl...she's escaped." Rainer tossed his head back and a deep throaty laugh bobbled out.

"Of course she did!" He was no longer laughing. "I don't even want to ask how she was able to slip out from underneath your nose."

"We had stopped to consult the map and she must have gotten a hold of a sharp rock... the ropes look like she was working on them for a while..."

"I said I didn't want to know, Quill. You have had your chance, get back to base camp! I should have known you would fail me."

"But, Sir, I can find her. She can't have gone far."

"You have *one* more chance Quill. One! If you don't get this little girl under control then I will have to step in, and, I assure you, that is *not* something you want." Rainer's voice was laced with venom. "I'm giving you two hours. Don't call me until you have her!" He spat as he yelled the words.

Storming back to the car Rainer grabbed one of the mercenaries closest to him by the collar.

"Are you as useless as the rest?" He demanded.

"No, Sir." The man answered, standing a head taller than Rainer.

"Good, I have a job for you."

13

STRUGGLE

A blast that sounded like thunder tore into the silence of dusk. Emily could feel the hot metal passing by her ear. The bullet embedded itself into the bark of a tree off to her left, splitting the wood. It had been a warning shot, she knew. If her pursuers had wanted to hit her she would have been dead by now.

Emily slowly pivoted on one foot; she was unable to see in what direction the shot had come from. In the cover of the trees it would be nearly impossible for her to see anything, but they had clearly displayed their ability to see her.

Her heart beat wildly in her chest and pounded in her ears, making it hard to listen for footsteps. The hunt was over; out of 'predator prey instinct' she knew she was done. Facing her own fragile mortality, a burst of adrenalin pumped into her veins forcing her to move. Stepping back, she almost lost her balance as the ground behind her sloped sharply downward. In the dim light of the setting sun Emily couldn't tell how far down the slope went but it gave her an idea. If she could only slip down and out of sight, maybe, just maybe, she could hide. She could survive the night.

The plan was failing, falling apart faster then the heavy breath coming from her lips. She could feel eyes on her, watching her every movement. Tentatively she scooted her right foot behind the left one and shifted her weight.

Then before Emily was able to run behind the tree, down the slope and into the darkness, another shot rang out. Emily threw herself to the cold ground so hard she knocked the wind from her lungs, and then lay not moving, not breathing. The shot had sounded distant, like it was going in the opposite direction. It had been out of pure fear she had thrown herself to the ground and now was frozen in place. Emily felt numb but her mind raced. Feeling dizzy, she allowed herself to take a deep breath. The air rushing back into her lungs was cold and the effort painful.

A few seconds later, she heard the faint sound of leaves crunching under boots. The sound died away as fast as it had come- then nothingness once more enveloped her.

Knowing that she couldn't stay there Emily risked lifting her head only a little, hoping to see or hear something more, yet the night still hid its secrets well. Unarmed, and in the covering darkness she would be blind to any movement. The nauseating feeling of being trapped, as if she was back in the caves, and helplessness overwhelmed her.

"Emily." As soft as a breath of wind her name floated over her. There was no need to look or make a guess of who had spoken her name and the knowledge started to comfort her. She sat back on her knees, squinting into the darkness for him.

"Kip?" A sound behind her forced her heart to stop, and then it happened so fast that Emily hardly had time to process even the smallest action. A large figure burst out of the woods, running at her full speed, and then grabbing at her arm with the momentum of a freight train forced her backwards and down the slope.

A terrified scream held itself in her throat but was never allowed to leave. In the back of her mind she knew that whoever held her was not one of her pursuers or she would have been dead.

Then, in an instant, her back hit solid ground and the wind was forced from her body once more. Head over heels, she tumbled down the steep incline of the slope, the grasp on her arm never relenting in its tight hold on her. She fought for air as the ground and sky melded into one circling mass of confusion. Gravity yanked at her unmercifully, the momentum forcing her to move faster and faster as the slope steepened. The tender flesh at her face, neck, arms and legs was being cut and bruised by rocks, twigs and branches that were all tearing at her.

The pain was only out done by the fact that she had yet to take a breath. Emily felt herself slowing down and the hand that had held her let go. She was now rolling down the last of the hill, somewhat as a child would, arms folded across her chest, legs out. By the time her body stopped she was positive that she had just fallen down a ravine, not simply a hillside, as she had thought before.

With more effort than she had known before, she forced herself to breathe. Emily's chest rose and fell in painful shutters. Reaching up with one hand she touched, very carefully, a tender spot near her hairline. The gash caused by the fall was deep, raw and bleeding.

Mind whirling, Emily lifted her head to look around; she had been grabbed by Kip, she was sure. But, where was he now? She also knew that even though she had not screamed on their decent that there could be no doubt their followers had heard the fall and would be upon them in a matter of moments. Fear slowly crept in between the aches and pains she now felt.

Trying to sit up an excruciatingly bright light burst behind her eyes and pain protested the movement.

"Emily!" Kip's voice reached her ears. Out of the darkening shadows to her left he was moving toward her, crawling across the muddy ground.

He was next to her, looking down at her, his features dull in the dim light. Tears sprang to her eyes and forced their way out. He touched her cheek with cold fingers. Then pulled her close to him.

"I wasn't sure, I thought you'd been hit..." his voice trailed off when his eyes moved to the cut on her head.

"It's from the fall," she whispered, answering his unspoken question. "I wasn't hit."

He looked deep into her eyes, his face so close that even in the pale moon light casting down through the trees she could make out the golden flecks in them. Emily wanted to put her arms around him and comfort herself in the warmth of his embrace, but she willed her arms to stay at her sides.

"I hoped that you would come," She admitted, "But it was a trap." Kip didn't respond for a moment.

"I'm sorry to jump on you like that, I didn't know how else to..."

"I was thinking the same thing- get down the hill and into cover. I was going to do it a little less dramatically then your way, I admit." Emily smiled at him but Kip did not return the smile.

"I'm sorry I left you, I should never...did they do anything to you? Hurt you?" Kip's eyes were searching her face.

"No, I mean they didn't hurt me, just kept me walking without food or water. I was able to cut my hands free, and as soon as I could I took off running. I didn't get very far. How did you find me?"

"I've been tracking them, trying to find a way to help you escape." Kip was staring at her in a way that made Emily want to blush. Then he cleared his throat. "We can't stay. Do you think you can walk?" His voice was low and raspy.

"Yes, it's just my head that hurts." Emily attempted a smile. "How about you?"

"It's just a graze." He said eyes casting to his left arm. It was then that Emily allowed herself to take in the rest of Kip's appearance. His shirt was cut at the sleeve and blood covered his shoulder. She hadn't noticed before, but he had been hit by the second gunshot. Everything else on them was now covered in mud and undergrowth. Kip had started to brush leaves from her hair, so gently, she hardly noticed. It was his eyes burning into her face that took her attention.

Emily was instantly aware of Kip, herself and the beating of her heart. He had pulled her closer to his side; there was more force in the tension of his fingers on her skin. Then, before Emily could react, Kip pressed his lips to hers.

Kissing Kip was painfully sweet and she answered his kiss with her own. It seemed like a lifetime before Kip pulled away from her. Emily no longer felt the pain in her body and was warm next to the coldness of the night. Yet, there was no time to relish in the exchange that had taken place between them.

The sound of falling rocks above their heads had pulled them away from each other. Kip looked up toward the sound, his jaw set, a frown creasing his lips. She knew what he was thinking without the words being said. Their time had run out.

****

Bernadette glanced out the windows of the cabin again and her fingers ached to open the door and find her friend standing on the other side. Her mind told her that Emily would not be there.

"Bern, stop. They're fine. I'm sure we'll hear from them before…"

"Before we have to leave?" She broke into Doug's sentence. "I can't just abandon her Doug! Emily would never leave me." Doug got up from his station in front of the computer and took Bernadette by the shoulders.

"We're too exposed if we stay in the cabin, besides I am done decoding the files. I'm downloading them now. Emily and Kip knew what they had to do."

"I know Doug. But now I feel…like I sent her out to the lions. How could I let her use herself as bait?" She turned to face him.

118

"Bern, look. None of us asked to do this, we didn't want this responsibility, but it's ours, and now seeing what I have seen, knowing what I know! We have to get these files copied and into the right hands. You know this." Bernadette was annoyed that he would lecture her about what she knew.

"It's not your best friend!" She snapped at him. "It shouldn't have taken them this long! Something's happened to them! We should have heard from them by now!" She was almost screaming at him.

"I'm sorry, I didn't mean to sound insensitive." Doug said, deep lines creasing his forehead. Bernadette didn't have time to respond as a soft beep came from the computer. Both turned to look at it, holding their breath. Then the words they had been waiting for flashed on the screen: 'transfer complete'.

****

Kip half carried, half dragged Emily along the rocky path. He was careful to keep their footsteps light and on rocks to leave as little trail as possible.

Night had completely fallen and it was getting harder to see their way. Neither said a word as they traveled.

A few more minutes went by, then just as Emily's eyes were adjusting to the new darkness, Kip ducked under a rock outcropping that she hadn't noticed. Now hunched over they were forced to slow their flight.

Kip stopped so suddenly that Emily ran into him. He motioned for her to stay quiet and seemed to be holding his breath. Then she saw it, a light, shining above them. More flashlights joined the first. She could hear three distinct sets of footsteps then the voices echoed down to their hiding place.

"No trail yet, Sir." Emily could hear the crackle of a radio. She was unable to make out the response, but the first man started to talk again.

"No Sir…" A pause. "Yes Sir. We found blood." Another response from the man on the radio. Emily felt herself straining hard to catch a word or two.

"Sir…No Sir, we had to call the dogs off…" Another pause. Emily felt herself shiver. Dogs had been put on their trail. She was still unable to hear the other man but his voice was now higher, clearly angry by this new development. "Rain, Sir... The dogs are crisscrossing… We'll find them, Sir."

It was then that Emily turned her face toward the tops of the trees in the distance. The night was so cold and dark because of the massive clouds that hung over the mountain.

The clouds had come up fast. Large droplets had started to fall in silent waves around them. Emily breathed a prayer of thanks. Without the scent being slowly washed away by the rain they would have been found in no time by the dogs. Their pursuers were close as it was, too close, and the thought made Emily feel trapped, like a wild animal.

Hunched in the tight space, crouched next to Kip, Emily could feel the exhaustion creeping up on her. They hadn't moved from their hiding place; the lights from the men above had long since moved away, back into the darkness, no foot steps, no voices. They were alone again.

Kip pivoted on one foot and reached to touch Emily. The warmth of the touch felt, somehow, unfamiliar to her.

"We need to keep moving, find a place to stay the night." Emily nodded. Kip started to walk again. Emily tried to move after him but her legs felt like stone.

"*Move!*" She screamed in her head as she clumsily trailed after him.

The outcropping of rock disappeared and Emily felt relief, as she was able to stand up straight, the cool rain pouring over her face. The ground was slowly sloping upward; she could feel the strain of it in her calves as she slipped her way up the trail.

"Are you okay, Emily?" Kip's voice reached her but she couldn't seem to process it clearly. Some place between the cold, the chattering teeth, the shooting pain in her head, the hunger gripping at her stomach, and lack of sleep, her mind had all but shut down. Emily stumbled. She wanted to reach out, to catch herself before she fell, but her hands hung at her sides, unable to find the strength to lift them up. Falling forward, her eyes closed as the ground came up to meet her, but she never felt the impact.

"Emily?" She could hear his voice, sounding so far away now that it wasn't more than a whisper to her. "Emily, can you open your eyes?" She was sure she was nodding. She tried hard to will her eyes open, but her eyelids felt so heavy, her whole body felt heavy.

"Emily…" Kip sounded closer to her now and something warm touched her skin. Emily wanted to open her eyes but the blackness of sleep pulled at her.

"Kip?" Her own voice sounded weak and strained to her ears. She wasn't sure she had thought his name or said it.

"It's okay, we've stopped for the night. You're safe." It was then that Emily realized that she no longer felt the rhythmic pat of rain on her face and body.

With considerable effort her eyes fluttered open. It was still dark, darker than it had been.

"Where?"

"It's okay, we're in a cave. Emily does anything hurt? Are you okay?" His face was next to hers, so close that she could make out his features clearly in the murkiness.

"I'm tired." She tried to smile but wasn't sure if her face would obey her. Kip seemed relieved.

"I wasn't sure when you started to fall…" His hand was touching her face, it was the warmth she had felt while someplace between sleep and awake. She felt herself shiver, but, not from the cold this time. "Sleep." His voice was strong and deep. The sound made her feel safe.

"You're not going to leave are you?" A strange sense of panic, that had nothing to do with the man that was looking for them, shot up her spin.

"No." His mouth was next to her ear. He lay down next to her, stretching the length of his body out next to hers. She felt his arms, strong and warm; curl themselves around her back, pulling her towards him. Emily lifted her head to rest on his shoulder, her face buried into his chest.

"Kip…" She mouthed. He didn't seem to notice. Emily wanted to tell him why her heart jumped and skipped at his lightest touch. To explain why her head spun anytime he was around, why her thoughts always seemed clouded when she thought of him, but thinking hurt her head even more than moving, and she wanted to sleep. There would be time for confessions and questions later.

Emily knew that she would have to find answers to his very mixed signals, but not now. Now, she was just happy to be next to him, breathing him in… then before she was able to question further, sleep found her.

****

Bernadette held her seatbelt strap tight to her chest as Doug took another sharp curve in the road. In the seat between them lay five small brown, thin packages, with her neat black letters spelling out names of news stations.

Bernadette found herself daydreaming of the last time she sat next to Doug driving down this very mountain. It seemed like a lifetime ago, before their first kiss, before Harold Pinchly, before the burden of knowledge that would change their lives forever.

"Hold on Bern, we're being followed." Doug's voice sounded strained and the words came through clenched teeth. She glanced backward and from the darkness came two pairs of headlights. They rushed toward their small Jeep. Bernadette glanced at Doug; his jaw tight with lines of stress. He gripped the wheel.

"How do you know they are following us? Maybe…"

"We passed them sitting on the side of the road waiting for us to make a move. They've been driving behind us with their lights off." Bernadette felt her heart skip.

"What do we do?"

"We run. We can't do anything else." Bernadette cringed at his words. They had no cell phones, no weapons, no way to fight back, nothing but the information they carried.

Lights flashed in the rear view mirror and lit up the cab of the Jeep. Bernadette gripped the seat as Doug sped around another corner, Bernadette said a silent prayer as they passed a sign warning drivers of the steep downward grade, steep drop offs and to beware of falling rocks.

A sudden jolt from behind confirmed Doug's assessment as one of the cars rammed them from behind. Doug swerved a little but was able to keep control of the Jeep. Bernadette was not able to keep a small sound from escaping her mouth.

"Hold on." Doug commanded and slammed on his breaks. The car behind him swerved to the left to avoid hitting them. In a movement too fast for Bernadette to comprehend Doug let off the breaks and jerked hard on the wheel, hitting the car hard on the side as they rounded another curve in the road, the mountain falling away to one side.

The sound of scraping metal filled the mountain pass. Then there was another sound as the first car; which had been unprepared for this sudden movement, went off the edge of the cliff. More crashing of metal, glass shattering, and rocks falling in cascades.

The second car sped up and their engine roared loudly in her ears. There was no way to get away from them this time. Doug grabbed Bernadette by the back of the neck and shoved her head down into her lap. She flung her arms over her head, hearing popping sounds she assumed were gunshots.

Doug swerved hard to the left as they rounded another curve in the road. There was another hard jerk to the back of the Jeep and more crushing metal. Doug fought to keep control on the wheel. They were going faster now, a steeper grade, Bernadette could tell without looking, as gravity played its part and pulled on her.

Then the light filling the cab faded as the car pulled along side of them. Both braced for what was going to come next. The jeep was thrown to one side hitting hard on rock. Doug fought his way back onto the road. The black car hit the Jeep's driver's side again and again forcing Doug and Bernadette into the rocky outcroppings. The driver would give Doug no chance to retaliate and surprise him as he had the first car.

The force of the black car was unrelenting as it smashed time and again into them. Bernadette knew they would not open fire again; they were wanted alive.

Bernadette pulled her head up a little. Doug was doing the only thing left to him, keeping the black car from getting ahead of them. They would be able to block the road if they pulled in front.

Once the information they were after was extracted from the Jeep, there would no longer be a need for either of them to live.

Doug sped up only a little, just enough to keep the car next to them, and as the black car slowed, so did Doug. Doug skillfully kept pace with the black car. There was no place for it to go and no time for anyone to stop what was already set in motion.

Suddenly, the road ahead filled the lights coming from the opposite direction. Something *big* was coming their way. The bright lights were followed by a semi-truck pulling a trailer. It was roaring around the sharp curve in the road up ahead and was coming towards them fast.

Bernadette felt the hairs on the back of her neck prickle with sudden, unspeakable, awareness of their situation. It was unavoidable for the semi not to hit one of the two cars barreling toward it. The semi driver slammed hard on it's brakes in a desperate attempt to stop. The momentum of the heavy load the driver was pulling was too much, as the wheels angrily gripped the asphalt, the rear end of the trailer started to fishtail viciously on the road. The wheels pulled hard to one side then the other, teetering precariously on the brink of a sharp drop off. The semi was screaming toward them, brakes screeching, the trailer pulled into Doug and Bernadette's lane.

Bernadette could see what was about to happen. Both vehicles side by side, did not have time to stop and would hit different ends of the semi-truck and trailer.

Then just seconds before the trailer whipped into their Jeep, a new sound erupted around them.

The tail end of the semi trailer was now scraping along side the mountain pass and slowly the rear tires lifted off the road. The scene was unreal, metal sparking, wheels spinning in the air as the gap between the trailer and road widened.

As the semi's cab came wheeling toward the black car the trailer was barreling toward their jeep. Bernadette forced herself to close her eyes, as Doug pulled hard on the wheel, heading for the small gap that was now forming between the road and the bottom of the trailer. He was going to try and skirt underneath the gap. Both pulled their heads into their laps as the world exploded around them.

The sound was like nothing she had ever heard before. She could hear the screams of tires on asphalt, the cries and moans of the crushed car, the force of the Jeep's soft-top being pulled from above as the semi's trailer passed over them. The smell of heat, sweat and rubber filled her nostrils. The feel of glass shattering, exploding around them, the thick canvas hit hard on her back as it was torn from above, peeling off like the top of a can.

Then, just as fast as it had begun, it was over and Doug was once again, desperately fighting for some control. Then the Jeep's wheels slammed into softer ground as Doug forced it onto an emergency exit ramp. The Jeep came to an instant stop.

Bernadette flipped around just in time to see the black car wrapped around the cab of the semi like an embrace. Then as the wheels finally found their grip and rolled to a stop, the black car, along with the front of the semi sat precariously close to the deadly drop off down one side of the mountain road.

The trailer had stopped its climb up the mountain's edge and teetered back and forth like a pendulum about to tilt to one side or the other. The truck's coupling seemed strained and made an awful noise as the trailer finally flipped onto its side, coming to rest on rocks and brush that covered the steep grade of the mountain road.

Bernadette felt hot tears streaking down her cheeks. Then, Doug's hand was on hers.

"It's over." He said. But deep down Bernadette knew that it was far from over.

****

Emily felt warm, warmer than she had in a long time. A slight breeze was pulling at her hair. Before she opened her eyes she could tell that daylight was pouring into the cave. Stirring a little, she found that she was still encircled in Kip's arms.

"Good morning." His lips breathed the words next to her hair. Emily pushed her head back and opened her eyes to look at him. Kip's face had been washed clean from the mud by the night's rain. His hair dark and glistening. He looked somewhat refreshed and rested. The worry lines that creased his face had eased.

"Hi." Emily choked. Suddenly, under his gaze, she was very aware of the fact that she had not cleaned up, that she had not been able to primp or brush her teeth before being so close to him, closer than she had ever been. But, his nearness felt normal, right, somehow.

"What time is it?" She asked, wondering how long he had let her sleep.

"Mid-morning. You needed your rest." His fingers traced the line of her jaw. Emily felt herself blushing under his touch. She wanted to look away from his dark creamy brown eyes, afraid that he would see her thoughts.

Suddenly before Emily could account for the change, Kip's eyes turned hard and dark. He shifted his body away from her and sat up. The action rolled Emily onto her back. She bit her lip. Once again, she knew, Kip had shut off.

"We're pretty close to an old Ranger station. They'll have a first aid kit for your head and maybe a radio." His voice was distant and disconnected. Emily sat up, pulling her knees under her, feeling very much alone.

****

Bernadette awoke in the back seat of the Jeep. They had stopped at the base of the mountain near an abandoned house to catch some sleep. She didn't want to open her eyes; if she did, last night would become real again and all she wanted to do was forget.

"We need to get a new car and a change of clothes." She opened her eyes. Doug was pulling all their things out of the Jeep. He looked like he had aged during the night. He slung his computer bag over one shoulder.

"There are a few homes in Shell where we can look for a vehicle. It's time."

He was right, it was time.

14

FRIEND OR FOE

Kip walked fast, not turning to see if Emily was able to keep up with him. She was working hard to keep him in her sight, but the undergrowth gripped at her feet and she kept falling against the nearby trees.

If she had not been so intent on watching his back as he moved ahead of her, wondering what she had done to make him so angry, she could have paid more attention to her clumsy foot steps.

"We're here." He said, not really looking at her. Emily looked in the direction he pointed. A small brown cabin, looking more like a hut that had been reclaimed by the forest than a cabin, stood off to their left and up a sharp hill.

Kip didn't wait for her, but with an energy that surprised her he bounded up the incline to the door. It gave way under the pressure of his good shoulder and he disappeared inside, leaving her to climb after him.

Once inside the doorway, it took a few minutes for her eyes to adjust to the dim light. Kip burst through a doorway off to her right, almost running into her.

"First Aid kits in the bathroom." He grumbled and stalked past her. "I'm going to see if the radio works." He walked over to the opposite side of the one large room that took up most of the space. Emily shut the cabin door behind her, blocking out a good portion of the sunlight. A few of the old wooden shutters on the windows had fallen aside and streams of light poured into the room. She left Kip, who was bending over some equipment, and walked into the small side room he had indicated.

The bathroom, as he called it, was the size of a small closet. An old porcelain sink stood next to the door. Above the sink in the place of a mirror, was the white and red first add kit. Next to that was a toilet and tiny shower. Neither looked like they had worked in years.

Emily shut the door, not wanting to hear or see Kip for a minute while she tried to make sense of so many things. Doug and Bernadette, the flash drive information, the hundreds of young women being sold into slavery, the men that would not be far behind them, and no place to hide. No place to go. It all should have been overwhelming; it should have been weighing on her, but at the moment the only thing she could think about clearly was the man brooding in the other room.

Suddenly Emily was angry too. She turned the handles on the sink, she wasn't sure that any water would come but was pleasantly surprised when the pipes rattled and water came splashing out.

She washed her hands, arms, and neck, then cooled off her face, flinching a little when she got too close to the cut on her forehead. Then with impatience that frustrated her, she tore open the first aid kit. The contents were sparse but she was able to find some painkillers, medical tape, and gauze. Then, close to the back, a small tube of antiseptic. It would have to do.

Emily still had the water running, afraid that if she turned it off it would not turn back on. She gingerly touched just below the cut- again wishing for a mirror so she could see what she was doing but filling her hands with water anyway, she splashed it on the wound and jumped a little.

"Emily? Is everything okay?" Kip's voice floated over her; she didn't want to answer him. She filled her hands again and repeated the action. The door pushed open a little, Emily still wasn't sure she could face Kip without bursting at the seams. Kip inched the door open, passed her and stepped in.

"Let me help." His voice was low again, low and smooth. The sound bothered Emily more than she would like to admit.

"No, I have it." Emily bristled a little. She felt her mood matching his from earlier. Behind her Kip grabbed her hand as she lifted it with more water. The cold liquid slipping though her finger tips and down her arm. His grip was like steel and he turned her to face him. The room was suddenly smaller than before.

Emily felt the air rush out of her. Kip's eyes blazed at her, reading her effortlessly. Without words he pushed her against the wall and with one hand on her arm, the other reached up and tore a small piece of cloth from his all ready torn shirt. He drenched the cloth in the cool water and lifted it to her face.

"This might hurt a little, try not to move." He said between clenched teeth but moved her hair out of her face with a gentle hand.

"Sure." Emily rolled her eyes a little, but he was right. When he started to clean the cut, it *did* hurt. Kip was gentle; more so than Emily would have guessed he could be. She didn't feel herself flinch under his gaze.

"Sorry." He muttered, sure that he had hurt her but Kip had no idea that Emily couldn't feel the pain any longer. He was leaning over her, his grip on her arm still held, but the fire in his eyes had changed. She found herself being lost in them.

Kip worked without saying anything else for a long time, until he seemed satisfied that the cut was clean. Then in a graceful movement, that Emily would have thought impossible for a man of his size, he grabbed the other items off the edge of the sink and went to work.

The antiseptic burned, Emily shut her eyes against the pain. Then a light tingle touched her skin, he was blowing air on the cut, and her eyes flew open. The sensation was powerful. But once again Kip seemed to be unaware of the affect he was having on her heart rate.

He let go of her arm, sure that she would stay put as he tore small pieces of tape off the roll. Then with skilled hands he placed them carefully to pull the two sides of the gash together. He placed gauze on top to keep it clean and more tape to keep the gauze in place. He was done.

Deep down Emily wished it had taken longer. She was feeling weak in the knees, glad for the support of the wall behind her. Kip was still so close she could feel his breath in her hair.

"You're shaking." He said so softly that she could have missed it.

"Sorry." Was the only thing she could think to say.

"I'm sorry that I hurt you." He must have thought her shaking was from the pain. Emily found the courage to look up at his face. New lines now creased it, lines of a sadness that she couldn't name.

"Your turn." Emily gulped and tried to smile.

Kip removed his long sleeved shirt with caution. Standing next to her in a t-shirt, that for her comfort level was just a little too tight, Emily was more aware of how small the bathroom really was. But, she pushed past the thought and took his left arm in her hands.

It was the first time she had seen the graze. High on his shoulder the bullet had cut it's way through the fabric and burned the skin underneath. Blood and soil matted together down his arm.

Emily took the same cloth Kip had used to clean her cut and rinsed it under the running water.

"I'll be careful." She set to her task, washing away the angry traces of their flight from the night before. It didn't take long before she was ready to move his shirtsleeve to get at the wound. With fingers that shook she pulled back the torn material to get a better look, glad that the shot had not been more exact in it's target.

In a few minutes it was as clean as she was going to be able to get it. With the little gauze, antiseptic and tape left, Emily wrapped his arm and started to clean up. All the while she trembled just a little. She analyzed her anger. It was anger at herself. It was clear now in her mind that she was the only one fighting with any kind of feelings.

Positive that the kiss had been motivated from the stress of the situation and nothing more, Emily remembered that Kip had walked away from her all those weeks ago. That he had let her know that she was too young for him, and he wanted nothing more to do with her. And now, alone with him, she had been stupid and let her emotions read his actions.

She felt foolish all of a sudden. But the feeling was overpowered by others. Emily knew she felt more for Kip than just the physical attraction. She was in love with him, with everything about him, and the realization angered her more than anything. Hot tears fought their way out of her eyes and Emily brushed them away with an angry hand.

"It's okay Emily. We'll find a way out of this." Kip must have seen this last desperate action of a woman on the edge.

"I was thinking of Doug and Bernadette." She lied. "I hope we have cleared the way for them to finish their part of the plan."

"Are you sure you're okay? Not going into shock? You look very… pale."

Emily set her lips in a hard line. She gave herself over to one more small moment of weakness and moved the short step that separated them and pressed her cheek to his chest. Kip's breathing seemed to stop for a moment. Then as a long breath escaped his lips, his hands gripped her shoulders.

"I'm okay, now." She breathed and then moved her own hands around his back, not caring that it might make him angry. He was making it more than clear that he didn't care about her the same way she had grown to care about him, but at the moment, she didn't care. Just needing to be close to him, to be in his arms.

"Oh," was all he said and he wrapped his arms around her small back. She had no idea how long they stood like that, but something was building up inside her chest. Then before she was able to stop it, or, before the words even registered inside her head they had spilled out.

"I really care about you... Kip. I... I..." But it was too late, he had shut down again. Pushing her away hard and dashing out of the bathroom. Emily stood stunned for a long while, then lips set into a thin line, jaw clenched she stormed after him. Kip was pacing the large room, his hands wringing though his hair.

"Did I do something wrong? I'm sorry I said anything. It was stupid. Please just forget it." Emily could hear that she sounded desperate, her voice high.

"I can't think!" He almost shouted at her, the veins on his neck seemed strained and all the muscles tight in his body, like he was fighting with something deep inside.

Emily wanted to run. She had never seen him like this. Then like a madman he turned on her, the blaze was back in his eyes, his face hard. "I can't think right when I'm around you! Everything gets all fuzzy and it's hard to focus." His stance relaxed and his head hung in a motion of defeat.

"Kip...I..." Emily gulped, confused about what was happening. He lifted his head up, dark brown eyes soft as silk now. He walked toward her in strides that seemed to take an eternity, stopping just a few inches from her.

"I think I'm over you, over feeling anything for you and then you get too close… or something reminds me of you, or the way you look at me and suddenly I can't seem to concentrate anymore." His hands balled up into fists. "Trying to keep us alive, keep one step ahead of the danger… trying to do what is right… then… there's *you*, and I can't seem to get you out of my head." Emily didn't know he had been fighting with himself so hard. She had been interpreting his distance as indifference.

"I feel out of control…" He whispered. "Bad timing." He grinned, a sad half grin.

"I had no idea." She really hadn't, and it shocked her that he would feel so strongly about her; that the feelings she had been fighting had not been one-sided.

Kip broke the invisible wall between them and pushed back a stray hair from Emily's cheek. "After the hospital I, felt… like nothing I had every felt before… for anyone…" He seemed to be having trouble forming the words. "I thought some time away would help me clear my head, then you came crashing back into my life and everything seemed to be moving so fast that I had no time to react..." He smiled again. "Not to you anyway." The sadness had left his eyes.

"You were so mean, so cold."

"This isn't the way I had imagined things happening." He said. "I was trying to push you away… to get you safely away… but you're stubborn." The smile went all the way to his eyes. "I'm really sorry about confusing you, treating you so badly. I don't have any excuses."

"But, if you felt something for me why did you want to push me away?" Emily asked still confused.

"I wasn't sure I could trust what I was feeling." He said honestly.

"Who was she?" Emily asked in a confident tone. Kip didn't ask how Emily knew but answered the question.

"Samantha and I where engaged for three years. We went to college together… she was amazing." Kip suddenly seemed to be very far away, his gaze moved from her face and locked on the wall opposite him. "I was mad about her."

"What happened?" Emily whispered.

"She wasn't as mad about me." Kip said with a tiny shrug. "Only weeks before the wedding she called it off. I didn't know at the time how blind I had been. Sam had been seeing one of my closest friends on the side. Looking back on things I should have known. I was never good enough for her, never ambitious enough, and Sam let me know it. She never supported me or what I wanted to do."

"I'm sorry." Was all Emily could muster. The air had been knocked out of her lungs. "The cabin? It was hers, wasn't it?"

"Yes. She's never been back." Kip looked back down into Emily's face. It felt like he was seeing her for the first time. "And until I met you I wasn't sure I would be able to let trust issues I had with Samantha go. I built up walls to keep people out, and hard as I tried I wasn't very good at keeping you out." Emily understood what Kip was trying to tell her and her heart raced.

"The kiss?" She asked.

Kip chuckled a little, "I was too relived to see you hadn't been hit, that you were okay. I would like to say I over reacted a bit, but to tell the truth it was more than that."

"More?" Emily asked, now braver she once again she closed the distance between them. Kip seemed to stiffen again as she did.

"I've been resisting the feelings I have for you from the time we meet." He said leaning away from her a bit. It was all becoming clear to Emily. All the little moments

136

they had shared had been just as real to him as they were to her. He hadn't been ready for a relationship, yet now he had stopped running had stopped turning off his emotions.

Emily reached out and took both his hands in her smaller ones and placed them on either side of her waist. Then before Kip could pull away, or object, she threw her hands around his neck and let them twist in his dark hair pulling him closer.

For a brief moment his eyes grew wide with surprise, then soft again. Emily bit down on her lower lip, not as sure of herself as she had been. Kip lifted one hand and cupped her chin, turning her face upward to look at him.

Her heart seemed to skip a beat as his lips brushed hers.

"I love you." She breathed against them. Again Kip grew rigid and Emily instantly regretted admitting the truth, even to herself.

Kip didn't push back this time and his grip on Emily tightened. She waited as he breathed in a ragged breath that sent shivers down her back. Then he kissed her again, this time with an intensity that Emily found herself matching. She melted in his arms. The kiss filling her up, healing a hole in her she hadn't known existed until that moment.

****

Bernadette glanced up and down the street. So this was Greybull? People bustled in and out of the small town's post office. No one seemed to notice them and slowly the knot in her stomach started to subside. Doug looked over at her and then took her hand in his. He smiled a little, a tired smile.

"Shall we?" Bernadette returned his smile and nodded. Their part of the plan was simple enough; get the evidence into the hands of the media. It was Emily she was worried about, playing the part of bait. She never checked in the night before and it wasn't setting well with Bernadette.

They started to cross the street, a warm breeze played around them and the sweet scent of roses filled the air. An elderly lady passed them as they walked toward the glass doors of the post office; there wasn't another soul inside the building that she could see. The thought occurred to her that they may just be able to pull this off and a real smile played on her lips.

As their footsteps reached the sidewalk Doug gasped a little, a strange sound that made Bernadette's bones ache, then he faltered and stumbled forward, one hand flying up to his chest. Images around her seemed to freeze in time as Doug pulled his hand away and found his skin stained with red. Bernadette's mind was unable to comprehend what her eyes were seeing. Her gaze met his and fear that she had never felt before tore at her insides. Doug once again stumbled forward, the breath being knocked out of his body by an unseen force. He crumpled onto one knee. A new red stain appeared on his shirt.

A scream ripped from her lips, so inhuman, so powerful that it hurt her ears. Doug now lay in a crumpled heap, one hand still in Bernadette's but face down on the concrete stairs.

"Doug!" She tried to call his name but it came out as nothing more than a muttered whisper. "Doug! Please!" Bernadette cried and moved to cradle his head in her hands, forcing him to look at her.

"I love you." The words formed on his gray lips. "I always have."

Bernadette sobbed, "Please Doug, get up, we have to..." but the words stopped in her mouth as tears took their place. He took a shallow breath, the pain clear on his face from the effort, the red spots that turned into pools and dripped from his shirt onto the pavement. "Help! Help me!" Her mind called the words out loud and clear.

Doug reached up a hand and slowly touched Bernadette's face.

"I love you." She managed to say between sobs. A smile turned up the edges of his mouth. "Please don't leave me, Doug… Please!" The light in his eyes were fading and the world once again seemed to creep in around them.

Other people's screams filled the air around them as bystanders realize what was going on. Bernadette could hear the sounds of tires screeching around a nearby corner. The sound reached Doug and with what seemed like all the strength he had left he yelled at Bernadette, his eyes wide.

"RUN!"

Then his hand slid from her face and lay lifeless at his side. Bernadette could hear the command in the word and with all the willpower she had she tore herself from Doug's body and raced up the remaining steps to the front doors of the post office.

Allowing herself a glance over her shoulder she saw the black vans, the armed men pouring out of them. Adrenalin pumped through her veins. She flew passed the doors and pulled out the brown envelopes from inside her jacket.

It was too late. Hands grabbed at her, seizing her from what seemed like all sides. The thin brown packages scattered on the floor.

"No!" Bernadette fought against her attackers but the large men held their grips like steal bars. She was being pulled back out of the building, past Doug, his face now gray and ashen. Bernadette tried to regain her feet and continued to struggle.

Then, something like fire tore at her body. Sound was impossible as a silent scream caught in her lungs, then small white dots played at her vision as the fire died down. Her eye's felt heavy and vision started to go black; before the blackness took her over, she saw two things at the same time; a taser gun being pulled away from her side and Doug's eyes, staring into nothingness.

"Dogs." Kip said next to her cheek.

Emily's eyes flew open, "That's not exactly the response I was hoping for." She said a little confused, looking up at Kip. He had become hard again; something unreadable in his eyes. Then Emily heard it too, dogs barking in the distance.

Then, suddenly, reality caught up with them. It was the sound that shook them out of each other's arms. Kip left Emily and rushed to one of the windows. He stood off to the side and poked his head just enough to one side to see without being seen by those outside.

"Emily!" His teeth were clenched so tight her name came out as a hiss. He was waving at her to get down and without question she fell onto all fours. Now it was her own heart that she could hear pounding in her ears.

"They're close... Too close..." Kip grumbled. Then a noise from the other direction caught their attention. A second group of dogs barked, sounding like they could have been in the same room.

Emily felt herself jump a little. She looked up to see Kip was also on the ground crawling toward her.

"Is there any way out of here besides the front door?" She whispered to him as he reached her.

"There's a back door this way. We'll have to be fast!" He motioned her to follow him. But they were too late and almost at the same time both doors flew open, flooding the room with sunlight. Emily blinked a few times as her eyes tried to adjust. She wondered why the men holding the dogs had not released them.

"Kip?" The voice came from a dark figure standing in the doorway.

"Mac?" Kip asked.

"Kip! It's good to see you old buddy!" Emily thought her brain was playing games with her but Kip was on his feet and the large man filling the door way entered the cabin and clasped hands with Kip. "We thought we might not find you." It was then that Emily realized the man Kip had called Mac was wearing a Ranger uniform. She felt her arms and legs turning into jell-o and collapse out of shear joy.

"Oh! Emily." Kip grabbed her and pulled her to her feet. He was smiling. "Emily, this is Mac, my boss's boss!"

"It's nice to meet you, but I wish it was under better circumstances. Let's get you two food and water then we can talk." Mac nodded to the men on the other side of the small room. They backed out leading the dogs with them.

Mac waved at Kip to follow him. "The cars are this way." He said and started down the slope away from the old ranger station.

Emily clung to Kip's side as they descended, not trusting her own legs to hold her any longer. Relief mixed with pain in her stomach. She wanted to jump and scream all at the same time. But, for now, she was happy just to walk next to Kip, in the sunlight and not look behind her.

****

Doors flung open, Bernadette could hear them but not see them, the pillowcase was still pulled over her head, her hands still tied behind her back. Lifted off her feet she was tossed bodily, hitting hard, hands unable to help her break her fall on to the hard cold surface.

"What do we do with her now?" A deep voice, she had not heard before, asked the question.

"She'll keep our other little friends company until we find out how much damage is done, then the boss will have to decide."

The doors closed with a bang, metal, she could tell by the unmistakable sound they made. Whimpers, something almost inhuman in their sound, crowded around her. Unable to see or protect herself, she shivered with the fear of the unknown.

"It's okay…" The words were spoken in a thick accent, Spanish. Tender hands pulled the pillowcase from her head. With her nose free from her encasement she took her first real breath and choked on the air. The smell was overpowering, filled with sweat and filth. The only light filtered in from the small crack between the doors.

It took a few more stench filled breaths before her eyes could focus. The air around her burned her eyes- urine- it was unmistakable.

With help from behind her she sat up and was able to take in her surroundings. It was the back of a truck. Crammed inside, standing, laying, sitting, it was filled with women, no, *girls* mostly; girls being sold into slavery. Slaves in the freest country in the world.

Bernadette guessed their ages ranged from as young as eleven to early twenties as far as she could tell. In the poor light she was able to tell that most of them were from Hispanic descent, but others, she was not sure about.

"You…hand?" The women asked in broken English, pulling on Bernadette's hands. Bernadette nodded.

She pulled on the ropes and, slowly, avoiding rope burn, removed them. Bernadette was grateful and smiled at her. Words still would not come to her. The grasp of what was happening was too far from her at the moment.

The truck lurched forward and sputtered. They where being moved.

****

The exchange in the Ranger Station had changed something in Kip that Emily could not explain, but rather liked. He never left her side, his strong arm around her shoulders was reassuring in its comfort. But it was more than that. The way he looked into her face had also changed. Emily wasn't sure she could put her finger on it but there was something glistening in his eyes that warmed her from head to toe.

"How long have you been out looking for us?" Kip asked Mac between slow gulps of cold water and a bite of a granola bar. Emily sat quietly as she worked on her own.

"Since last night." Kip gave Emily's shoulders a knowing squeeze. He must have been thinking the same as she was. It had been them last night, not their pursuers.

"Mac. Look, this is big and we need some help." Mac held up a hand.

"Are you talking about running from a crime scene, or aiding and abetting a criminal?" He raised one eyebrow.

"It's a lot more complicated than that." Kip reached into his shirt and pulled out a long chain, on the end was a black flash drive. Emily's eyes grew wide in spite of herself. She had thought Bernadette and Doug had the only copies of the files. Mac took the flash drive from Kip and turned it over in his hand

"We need to get you off the mountain and then we can go over all this. For what its worth, I know you had nothing to do with the death of Alston or that other man. This will be okay, Kip, I promise." Mac placed a hand on Kip's shoulder and looked him in the eye as he slipped the drive into his pocket.

"I will do what I can. Trust me." Emily felt the sip of water she had taken turn into ice in her mouth. Had Mac just said "Alston"? How could he know that Senator Alston was in any way connected to them? It would make sense that the press would have released the names of both Harold Pinchly and Landry Alston on the news but only someone, someone involved would know of their connection to Kip and Emily.

Kip's grip on her shoulder had suddenly become painful and Emily knew without saying a word that Kip's train of thought had gone to the same place. She didn't dare look at his face for fear that her calm exterior would shatter like glass. Before either were able to say or do anything a younger Forest Ranger rushed up to the three of them.

"Mac!" He panted. "Mac, I just got off the radio with the Sheriff. There's been a shooting in Greybull." Emily suddenly felt the ground move, Greybull… Greybull… where Doug and Bernadette would be. "A man was shot and killed, the women he was with was seen being taken, kidnapped they think." He was talking fast and Emily's mind was skipping words trying to keep up.

"Have they been identified?" Mac asked, there was a glint in his eye that made Emily's stomach lurch.

"She fits the description of the woman suspected to be involved in the Billings airport killing." Emily rushed to the side of the truck, the water and granola spilling from her mouth. She was unable to stop the dry heaves that followed or from tasting the bile that filled her mouth.

"They killed him!" She sobbed, dropping to her knees. "They killed Doug and she's gone! Bernadette is gone!" Words soaked with tears came pouring out. After that nothing Emily cried was coherent until the tremors left her body. Then she sat, cradled in Kip's arms, he was whispering in her ear.

"It's okay. Love, it's okay." But something in his voice told Emily that he didn't believe the words either.

****

Bernadette sat with her knees curled up underneath her chin- eyes burning- tears welling up in her eyes.

144

The girls crowded into one corner, holding onto each other as the truck bounced along. Sobs, words in their native tongue, cries that went unheard by everyone but Bernadette. They filled her ears to the point that she felt her head was splitting in two.

She had no idea how long any of the girls had been trapped but it was long enough that they had been forced to relieve themselves, living in their own excrement.

No hint of cool air in the hot human oven, no food, no water. The smell of death was all around her, it stuck to her skin, soaking into her pores. She sat in things she could not name and did not care to know.

Sitting in the back of the truck, she let her mind wander back to the small town, back to Greybull, back to the post office steps. Her mind went back to Doug, his face gray, blood pooling, his tall frame crumpled on the steps. Bernadette felt her soul ache with a depth that she had not known that she had.

Then it was more than the heat, the smell, the filth, it was the loss she felt. The loss of a love that would never be in full bloom. She had loved him, falling for him deeply and now... now she cried. She cried with the true pain of despair, racking her frame with sobs that erupted from deep inside and, beyond her own power, forced their way out of her. For a time, all other feelings slipped away- and she let herself feel the true depths of her desolation.

****

Emily sat in the back seat of Mac's Ranger vehicle, Kip in the front. Mac had sent the other two with the dogs on ahead of him. Emily didn't have to guess why. He was being paid off, she was sure. He *knew* about the connection to Senator Alston and didn't blink at the news of Bernadette's kidnapping or the murder. Now he was talking to Kip as if they were on a Sunday picnic, not hunted and wanted individuals.

145

"We'll get you two handed over to the proper authorities and I am sure all of this mess can be worked out." Mac was chatting on.

"Back there, you said something, something about Alston." Kip said his voice laced with ice.

"Sure, why?"

"I was just wondering how much they are paying you. How much are our lives worth?" Kip had turned in his seat to look at Mac.

"Paying me? What are you talking about?"

"Mac, I never said anything about Alston and there is only *one* way you could have known he was connected to the killing at the Billings airport, or to us. So I want to know if the money you are getting to betray a friend, yourself, and to corrupt your morals and standards is really worth it?" The air between the two men became electric with the stress in Kip's every word. Then it happened so fast Emily wasn't sure what she was seeing. Mac reached for something and at the same time Kip grabbed the wheel, yanking it hard to the right.

Emily wished she had been able to scream, to close her eyes and brace herself for the action that followed. The truck started to fish tail out of control as the two men fought. Then, before anyone had time to react, the back wheels hit an incline on the side of the dirt road sending the truck bed into the air.

All at once she felt weightless and time seemed to work in slow motion. Emily waited for the tires to hit gravel again and the world to make sense. Instead, the front tires screeched to the edge of the road, a rolling hill full of rocks and trees staring up at her, they seemed to pause at the point of falling when the truck tipped and rolled.

There was screaming now, so much Emily was sure it could not be coming from just one person. Glass popped and rained all around her, her stomach turning at the sound of metal grinding on rock and breaking branches. Then the screaming stopped and so did their descent. The truck came to a abrupt stop as the bed tried to wind itself around the base of a tree. Steam and falling bits of debris filled the air.

Gravity had come back and was pulling hard on her. Hanging from her seat belt in the back seat, Emily coughed, spitting out blood mixed with saliva. Raising her hands over her head she pushed on the roof of the truck, the hard ground pushed back. She could hear the truck still settling into its new resting place.

"Emily?" Kip was reaching for her from the front seat; he favored his non-injured arm as he crawled from the front to her side. "Emily, we have to get out of here." He was pulling on her seat belt. But her eyes had adjusted and had locked onto Mac's form in the driver's seat. So still. This was not right, not right, a person's skin was not supposed to be that color. His eyes should be looking back at her in the rear view mirror not glassy like a doll's. Her seat belt gave way and Emily crashed head first on to the hood. Emily couldn't take her eyes off Mac as she righted herself in the cramped space.

"He's dead." Kip said in a matter of fact tone that sent chills over Emily's body. "Broken neck." It was Kip's voice again, but now farther away. Emily had turned from him, from those glassy eyes and was crawling out the broken window, grasping at roots and dirt to pull herself out. Once out, she fell to her knees, heart beating fast, and the world spinning.

It was happening to her all over again. Harold Pinchly, and now, Mac. Flashes of images she was repressing forced their way out.

"Emily." Kip was calling to her, then he was next to her, holding her. "Emily its okay honey." Kissing her hair, cheeks, and forehead. She took full deep breaths then pulled away from his embrace.

"I'm okay, Kip." She said, and it was true. "I'm okay." She glanced back toward the truck, lying on its hood, broken against the tree. "He was your friend. I'm sorry Kip." Then she looked at him, this man next to her. It felt like she had never really seen him before.

Once again something had changed in him. So much had happened that she was sure neither of them were the same people they had been two days ago. Kip stood and walked back to the truck. She watched as he took a small flash light out of the glove box then he went over to the driver's seat and bent down. Then he was back, holding out his hand to Emily. She took it and noticed the flash drive in his other hand.

15

CAPTIVE

Bernadette could hear voices, harsh words being spoken on the other side of the doors. She found herself huddled closely with her companions in the dark space. Bright sunlight streamed into the truck as the doors were flung to the side.

"All of them." One of the voices barked the order. Others stepped into the back of the truck and started to place burlap bags over the girls' heads. No one fought back, no one cried or said a word. Bernadette got the feeling that none of it would have helped anyway.

She was grabbed along with the others, a bag placed over her head. Her hands were left free at her sides as they pushed her out of the truck and into waiting arms. Tossed roughly to the ground by the second man, she stumbled and fell to one knee. She got back on her feet as rough hands grasped at her, pushing her forward. Within a few steps she was once again plunged into darkness, no sunlight bleeding through the cover on her head.

"Stop them here." This new voice was a deep base, so deep in fact it almost sounded unnatural. A door was shut somewhere nearby and the bag was torn off her head. Bernadette blinked a few times, her eyes adjusting to the dim light in the large room. It took a few seconds for her to realize that she was standing in line, girls on both sides of her, in a warehouse, and, before her eyes had fully adjusted, she saw the large bulk of the Giant standing off to her right. He was grinning in a sinister way. His one good eye found her and the smile widened.

"Get them ready." It was his voice she had heard. That was odd. She had expected the Giant to have an accent, not this extraordinarily deep voice. He moved from the shadows and came to stand right in front of Bernadette. She glared up at him.

"Hello, Little One. You have been causing us all kinds of problems, haven't you?" The Giant said. He was amused by this and shook his head. "It's a shame really." He said more to himself than to her. Then she heard the sound of electric razors whirling. The Giant must have seen the look of confusion on her face.

"Our last inventory had lice. This is an easy and simple way to relieve ourselves of that problem." He was scanning her with his one good eye and making Bernadette feel as if all the filth that was on her was somehow seeping into her skin. In the dim light she could see the locks of hair hit the ground, discarded.

"What are you going to do with us?" Bernadette demanded in a voice that didn't sound like her own.

"Us? No, there *is* no *us*. *You* will be coming with me." He said bending close to her face. She could smell his hot breath and feel it moving her hair. "We have a date, you and I. The others will be cleaned up and, well, I'm sure, no, positive, that you read over the documents on the flash drive, so I won't bother wasting breath lying to you in regards to what will happen next. But most of these girls will be spending their days sewing your great American fashions." He fingered the sleeve of Bernadette's torn shirt. "Other's have been sold to private individuals and, well, I'll let your imagination take over from there." He laughed at her. The sound was more of a low growl than a laugh and it turned her stomach.

"This one too, Boss?" The question came from a male voice someplace behind her. Bernadette had seen them shaving the hair off the women's heads, one by one, down the row. The Giant seemed to think about this for a few moments. He reached out and

150

pulled on one of her curls, letting it go to spring back into place. Fixing her with in his gaze he smiled again.

"Yes, her too." The Giant turned away as the man pushed Bernadette's head down roughly and she felt the razor meeting the back of her neck. There was no protective layer between her skin and the razor and as her hair fell down around her feet she could feel the razor biting into her head from time to time. She refused to let the hot tears of anger that were building up run free. She would not give the Giant that kind of satisfaction.

****

Emily felt her legs freeze underneath her. No, it couldn't be… not the same one. She felt like she couldn't trust her eyes anymore.

"Kip?" Her voice was tired and odd sounding to her ears.

"You are going to stay here, I'll be back." He had turned her to face him. "Emily, you know it will be faster for me to go on my own. I have to try and this is the safest place for you to stay. You can't be out in the open and there isn't any other place." They had talked about Kip going to find help but she hadn't dreamed in a million years that he would bring her here to wait for him. The mouth of the cave hadn't changed; it was the same one she saw in her dreams, gaping, black, and ready to swallow her whole.

"There isn't any other place." He was still talking to her.

"No! You can't ask me to go in there by myself!"

"Just far enough to not be seen." Kip pushed the flashlight into her hand. "I don't want to leave you, but…"

"They'll be looking for both of us." She finished for him, understanding. Then something caught her eye over Kip's shoulder that sent her heart racing. "Run!" She whispered to him, her eyes wide with fear. Kip did not turn to look; he knew what had scared Emily. He pushed something small into her hand, then pushed her hard away from him and dove into the woods. Emily had prepared herself for this and was running toward the caves full speed, the sound of Quill's laughter ringing in her ears.

Emily kept running down the jagged path that spilled into the large cavern where her spelunking class had stopped to rest. It seemed like a lifetime ago now, but here she was again, flashlight bobbling in her hand as she danced on bruised and unsteady legs around curves in the narrow cave path. Her mind was racing fast; if Quill was following her, then she had only one chance to get him good and lost in the cave. She had to calm down and think. The main cavern opened up in front of her. Emily pushed herself to the other side without looking back. A light flashed behind her in the cavern.

"You're making this harder than it has to be." Quill's voice was full of mirth. Emily shut off her light as she ducked into the tunnel leading out of the cavern. There was nothing like the fear that was pumping in her veins now. She was being chased in the same place that haunted her dreams and this time she didn't have anyone on the outside guaranteed to miss her and come looking for her.

"Come out and play," Quill was pleading with her in a mocking tone. "I promise we just want to talk...for now." He was laughing at her this time.

Emily gulped and started to crouch down, trying desperately not to make a sound as she crawled away from the main cavern and Quill. She didn't dare turn on her light until she was past a few curves in the cramped tunnel. Nothing looked like it did in her dreams; but she could taste the moist earth with every breath, the distinct taste had never left her memory.

This was not the same, she realized. Before being left behind, she really hadn't paid much attention to where they were.

Emily heard something moving behind her, she turned off her light and holding her breath moved faster on her hands and knees. The caves were colder than she remembered too. Maybe that was why she wasn't able to stop trembling, she told herself, but knew that it wasn't true. All the darkness, the smothering blackness that had made her panic before, was twice as bad knowing Quill was on her tail.

She reached a fork in the tunnel and took a shaky breath. This was it, where she had made the same decision just months before. Right or left.

Emily shouted at herself mentally to get a grip on herself and focus! She had gone right- yes, right. Emily turned her light on and looked down both forks then started left. This time she was hoping that Quill would be following her; just far enough back to give her time. This time Emily was going to save herself.

The second fork was close. This fork had taken her into a tunnel that must have caved in at one point because it became small, too small to even move in. So, she had to back track and go right. She pointed her light down the tunnel. That is where she had fallen. Emily pushed herself to move. Quill would not be far behind her and even though she was telling herself to stay calm, or her plan would not work, just being back in the cave was putting an emotional stress on her body that was stiffening her limbs and forcing her to take shallow breaths.

Emily screamed at herself to keep going forward. Her wavering light showed the edge of the tunnel floor. Emily took one look over the edge before she dropped her flashlight over the precipice and turned around. She knew she probably only had seconds before Quill would be turning the corner and prayed she had enough time.

Jamming herself into as small a space as her body would fit, Emily held her breath and did the only thing she could, wait. It couldn't have been more than a few minutes, minutes that seemed like hours in the darkness. Emily felt panic seeping through her, its icy fingers gripping her heart. The urge to run was almost overwhelming. Then she heard it, the sound of his heavy breathing and the scraping of rocks.

Then the beam of his flashlight turned the impenetrable darkness into a murky gray. Emily felt terrible as the gray become lighter and lighter. She closed her eyes and prayed. Her hearing seemed heightened as the other senses dulled. Quill was moving past her hiding spot and going for the bait. She could hear him moving up the right fork.

Then, she made her move, slowly and deliberately creeping down the tunnel. Quill was not far down the left fork as Emily crept up behind him, matching his movements exact. As he got closer to the drop off and her flashlight, Emily braced herself for what she had to do next. Quill glanced over the edge and at the same instant Emily pushed forward with all her might, shoving her shoulder into him.

He made a funny sound in the back of his throat, and then yelled as his balance was lost and the large man tipped over the edge. Emily wished she had covered her ears. She listened to the scream, bones crunching against rock, and then nothingness. Emily didn't bother looking. She turned around and started crawling back.

****

Emily's eyes started to adjust to the changing light as she reached the mouth of the cave. There was no plan now, her mind was numb, almost like her senses had been overloaded and were now shut down.

"Miss Rivers, the drive please." Startled by the smoothness of the dark voice, Emily found herself surprised she was able to feel anything at all. She still couldn't see who was talking, but as she moved in the shadows of the cavern entrance he stepped into view. Tall, lean, powerful. His black hair gleamed in the sunlight, tailored suit looked very out of place in his current surroundings. Flashes of memories filled her mind, like

154

still pictures that held some clue in them. She wished she wasn't so tired and could focus.

"Emily." Her name coming from his lips gave her a very unpleasant feeling. "Emily, it's time to end this." Although he didn't attempt to move closer to her, one white hand stretched toward her, long fingers uncurling.

"Don't do it!" Emily jumped at the sound of Kip's voice. Her eyes darted around trying to locate him. The white hand moved, fingers flicking, and Kip was shoved into the path from behind tall pine trees. He was bloody, bruises appearing all over his arms and face, one eye cut, and so swollen that already, he was unable to open it. Behind him four armed men crept out of the cover of the forest. Emily couldn't seem to stop her feet from moving toward him, stepping into the light.

"That's a good girl." The man in the suit said coolly. "Now give me the flash drive." He stepped closer to her, his shoes kicking up a small cloud of dirt, marring his polished black shoes.

"No." Emily whimpered, her eyes still on Kip's face. The man in the suit smiled, a thin hard smile, and without looking back over his shoulder, he nodded. One swift abrupt nod, but it was enough of a message for his men to jump into action. One of the armed men pointed his gun to Kip's head, his hand on the trigger. Two others grabbed Kip at the arms and held him as Emily watched in horror as the fourth kicked Kip in the ribs.

"You grossly underestimated me and my resources. These men are but a part of a much bigger team. I am sure, by now, you have heard of the death of one of your friends and subsequent capture of the other." He leaned closer a grin parting his lips. "At least some of my men can follow directions." He nodded to the men off to his right again and Kip's beating started again.

155

"Stop!" She screamed and lunged forward, needing to stop the sound of bones snapping and Kip's groans of pain. Emily didn't make it a full step toward him when fire erupted through her right shoulder. She fell backward with the force, red staining her shirt. Everything seemed to move in slow motion. Emily looked at the man in the suit, a small gun clutched in his hand; those white fingers curled around it. He was no longer smiling.

"You have forced my hand." He was talking, she was sure, but the pain in her shoulder was all she could think of as it spread down her arm and through her back. He was kneeling next to her now, looking down with a look that could only be described as satisfaction in his eyes. Those eyes! Those icy blue eyes! Emily remembered. She had seen him before, standing on a corner in Lovell as they drove through town headed for the mountains. She would never forget his eyes, and suddenly, she knew, he also remembered her.

"That's right, you led me right to you." He said sneering, and slammed his foot onto her injured shoulder. Emily wanted to scream but only a squeak of pain escaped her lips. .

"A little trail of bread crumbs for me to follow." His breath on her face made her feel dizzy with sickness. "You should never have taken *my* property from Mr. Pinchly. Now you'll all pay for that mistake." Emily could feel his cold hands on her, feeling for the flash drive. He found it, the small lump in her pocket. The thin hard smile came back.

"There you are." He pulled it out and clasped it between pale fingers. Emily was only vaguely aware of anything but the heel of his shoe digging into her shoulder. Her vision was starting to become blurred, feeling each heartbeat as it forced blood out the wound in her shoulder.

****

Someplace between the glaring sunlight and the fuzzy blackness behind her eyelids, she imagined voices, so many voices off in the distance, no, not so far away, but closer now. Too many talking all at once. Then colors. Emily tried to force her eyes to focus on the colors and make sense of it.

"Miss Rivers?" Out of the sea of color a gray face stepped forward. The features cleared.

"Professor Stevens?" Emily was confused and closed her eyes. Why would he be in heaven? She was sure that was where she was. She had died, hadn't she?

"Emily!" Kip's voice she thought. Then he was next to her. This is what heaven was supposed to be like. Not the face of her old college professor. "Emily talk to me!" His voice was demanding and hard. Emily didn't like it. She tried to move; to ask him why he was being mean again, but with the movement came the pain. Sweet, clarifying pain. As the cobwebs swept aside, Emily opened her eyes.

"It *hurts*." She said smiling. "It feels good." Kip, looking like he had been put through a meat grinder, was scanning her face with his one eye.

"It feels good?" He asked.

"Yes. It means I'm still alive." She answered him.

"I've contacted the authorities." It was Professor Stevens' voice again. Emily realized that standing all around her, with looks of shock, horror, and confusion were local college students. That must be the colors she had been trying to focus on, their T-shirts. The normal seemed so out of place.

"Thank you, Professor," Kip said, his tone saying so much more than the words. Professor Stevens took off his plaid over-shirt and knelt on the ground next to Kip, pressing the cloth to the wound on Emily's shoulder.

"Where? Where did they go?" She asked and tried to sit up. The fire was back in her shoulder.

"Don't move." Kip pushed her back to the ground. "When the three van loads of kids showed up out of nowhere, all of them disappeared into the woods. Probably too many bodies to deal with." Emily understood what Kip meant. There were at least forty students looking down at the two of them. Quinn's men had been equipped to "deal" with two or more, but it would have left a much bigger trail to deal with than just the two of them becoming 'lost' or having some 'unfortunate accident'.

"Kip, he has the drive!" Emily felt panic spreading into her limbs.

"It's okay, Emily. It was a decoy. Doug…before we left the cabin he gave it to me. *Just* in case." *Good old Doug*, Emily thought.

****

Sunday July 20th

Bernadette was positive she had never fallen asleep, her eyes were glued on the wall across from her. She sat, back pressed against the legs of another girl. It had been hours, hours that they had been left in the warehouse; maybe even over night, she couldn't be sure. The only tell-tale sign that a significant amount of time had passed was the hunger pangs in her stomach and the aching of all her muscles.

Then, as promised, the Giant returned for her. He grabbed her by the arm and pulled her onto her feet without a word. Bernadette wasn't sure she could even hold up her weight anymore but it didn't matter. The Giant half carried, half dragged her into a smaller room across the warehouse. She was sure it must have been an office at one time, because it was the only place in the warehouse that had a window. Light streamed into the room from small fissures in the black paint on the glass.

158

"Sit." He commanded and pushed her toward a chair. "Tie her down." Another man, someone she couldn't see, did as he was told, tying her arms and legs to the chair. The Giant was arranging things on an old desk near the only other light source in the room, a bare bulb, and his back to her.

"Done, Sir." The man behind Bernadette said.

"Leave us." The Giant commanded and turned to face Bernadette. He held a small syringe in one hand, pointing it into the light so the liquid inside gleamed. He saw Bernadette eyeing it and smiled.

"This one will help you to remember, to *talk*." He said, coming a little closer to her. Then he seemed to rethink it and put the syringe back down. Instead he took up a different one, smaller. "This one will help you to *forget*." Once again he placed it back down. "This one is so painful you'll *wish* you could tear off your own skin." He showed her a third. Then, grabbing second to the last, and largest syringe, he grinned, and brought it close to her face. "And you have seen *this* one in action." The flame tattoo rippled as he flexed and a small amount of the liquid sprang out the end of the needle. Bernadette felt bile creep up the back of her throat. She knew rather than guessed he was referring to what happened to Pinchly.

"What do you want?" She screamed up at him. "You have all the disks, you have all the information. What do you think I can tell you that you don't already know?"

He lifted an eyebrow, "Did you think I brought you here to get information out of you?" Then he laughed and Bernadette knew how this was going to end.

She wanted to cry, to cry because she had lost everything. Doug was gone; she had no idea what had happened to Kip or Emily. The disks were gone. No one would know why she had died. Would they even be able to identify the body? Bernadette closed her eyes, sick panic tearing at her insides.

"I won't tell you what this one does. It's a personal favorite and I would rather *show* you."

She felt a hard prick in her left arm and she waited for death. But death didn't come. No, it would have been a welcome relief from the violent shutters, ear-splitting screams, rib breaking retching and searing pain that she endured following the injection.

After what seemed a lifetime, her eyes opened again to the bare bulb, swinging above her head. Bernadette could taste the bile in her mouth, smell the filth and stench of burned flesh. Then he was coming at her again, this time with a different syringe and Bernadette felt herself being pulled back into the darkness, pin points of light dancing before her eyes. She smiled into them, eyes rolling back into her head as the seizure began.

16

DISTORTED PRECEPTIONS

The world had ripped open at the seams. It felt as if every person cried out in a voice so loud it drowned out the sound of the explosion. Light spilled in, filling Bernadette to the brim. She could see the light from behind her closed eyelids. She wanted to open her eyes to welcome it but was unable to move. The screams had stopped and there was a new sound, far away popping sounds, yelling, accompanied by a voice that was almost reassuring in its authority.

"Medic!" Someone yelled so close to Bernadette she was sure it was right in her ear. They didn't have to yell; she could hear them talking just fine. Talking, but not talking to her.

"Is she alive?"

"Yes." Hands, two sets of hands cutting at the ropes that held her to the chair, pulling them loose. Bernadette felt the heaviness of her eyelids lifting and was able to open her eyes just enough to make out shapes moving around her. The Giant was on the floor, twitching, his arms and legs flailing in different directions. The wall behind him gone. She wasn't sure if she was dreaming as his body was flipped over and the light gleamed off a syringe poking out of his arm.

The sun was bright. Her mind moved so slowly that it was hard to make sense of what she was seeing. The men in black kept moving around, so fast, she wished they would stop moving, stop just for a while so she could understand what was happening.

161

"Where *is* that medic?" One of them was still yelling, so close to her ear that his voice was hurting her head. A different man, dressed in black, turned from her to look out the hole in the wall, a hole she didn't remember, or had it been there before and she hadn't noticed? Nothing made any sense, and then… it did. She squinted as her vision blurred again, FBI, that's what was printed on the back of his vest, FBI. She knew what that meant, Bernadette was sure she knew…knew something… but it was just out of her reach, and her head hurt so badly. The light was too bright. Too bright. She closed her eyes again. Yes, this was better.

****

Tuesday July 22nd

Emily pulled a chair next to Bernadette's hospital bed and sat down. It had been over two days and her friend had not opened her eyes. The Doctors said she was in some kind of drug-induced coma.

Emily frowned at the tubes going in and out of Bernadette, feeding her body and helping to flush her system of the poison she had been pumped full of. She prayed it would be enough to bring her friend back to her. Taking her hand, Emily leaned forward.

"Hey, girl. You need to wake up and talk to me. They tell me that you can hear me, I hope you can." Emily felt silly, not knowing what to say in this one sided conversation.

"I was so worried when we couldn't find you. Days of not knowing…" Emily pushed down the lump of emotion that had welled up in her throat. "The FBI along with some Rangers pulled Quill out of the cave and with in minutes had him turning on his own men. That's how we found you." Emily felt strange telling Bernadette about her rescue.

162

"Your family is here, your mom hasn't left your side." Emily whispered and glanced toward the couch where Bernadette's young mother slept, her mass of curly hair reminding her of the waves that used to adorn Bernadette's head.

"She is great and your dad is a rock." Emily gulped back the tears that showed in her voice. "Please! Please open your eyes. Fight…" Her voice was cracking with emotion. "Doug… Doug would want you to open your eyes, Bernadette." It was too much; the salty tears were spilling down her face and onto Bernadette's hand. Emily didn't try to say anymore, she couldn't. She just held her hand until the tears had been spent.

"How is she?" Emily didn't have to look up to know that Kip was standing next to her, his shadow laying itself over her like a cloak. She wiped away the remaining wetness from her cheeks.

"The same."

"She's a fighter, Emily." It seemed like Kip wanted to say more but had said everything in one sentence. Emily smiled a little and nodded her agreement. Kip bent and kissed her lightly on the head, then was gone, knowing without words that Emily needed to be alone.

"Miss Rivers?" Emily turned to see one of the government agents that had been involved in Bernadette's rescue, in the doorway.

"We need to ask you some additional questions." The agent said in a tone and brooked no argument. Emily nodded. It had been like this since they had been taken off the mountain. After what the government called "appropriate time" to have their injuries taken care of, Kip and Emily had been separated and questioned for hours.

Their statements were taken down, photos gone over, bargains made. After all, they had fled the scene of a crime and spent days running from police. No jail time for all three, as long as they testified against the persons implicated in the documents recovered from Doug's computer and the mercenaries involved in their kidnapping and Bernadette's torture.

After Quill had been recovered from the cave he couldn't seem to stop the flow of information that poured out of him. It was a ploy to get his own sentence reduced. He was more than willing to point fingers in any direction, as far as Emily could tell. His information had helped to capture three of the four men that had worked with him on the mountain and he had pinpointed the warehouse Bernadette was being held in.

Rainer, the man in the suit, she had learned his name, had still to be found. Emily doubted that he ever would be. He seemed the kind of man that could disappear, if needed.

Emily gave Bernadette's hand a squeeze, "I'll be back." She promised. Then Emily got to her feet, protectively cradling her right arm as she did. The sling was obnoxious at best, but kept her from moving the injured shoulder as it healed. The gunshot had been clean and had gone through her shoulder producing little damage.

"This way please." He said and she followed him down the hallway and into a small side room of the hospital which the FBI had commandeered during their investigation. Emily sat down, and prepared herself to revisit her worst nightmare again, for the record.

****

Emily rubbed her temples, fighting a headache as she walked out into the hall.

"Something to drink?" She was glad to see Kip leaning on the opposite wall, a tall glass of juice in his hand.

"Thank you." Emily took it from him gratefully.

164

"Come sit down," Kip said, placing a hand on the small of her back and guiding her toward a small sitting area. Emily took a sip of her juice and sank into a soft chair.

"Are you okay?" She asked Kip as he took the seat next to her.

"How are you?" He was putting off answering her question by asking one of his own. Emily let him have it.

"Holding up." This was fallowed by a long pause. Emily could tell Kip wanted to say something, she reached over and took one of his hands in hers. Giving him the opening to do so.

"I'm not sure how to go about this." He said. Emily could see the hard lines around his eyes coming back.

"I'm not Samantha, Kip." She lifted her face to his, her green eyes sparkling. "You don't have to keep me out you know. I'm not her."

What ever it was that Kip was going to say was lost in the kiss he placed on Emily's lips.

"We don't have to figure everything out right now."

"I can't promise you anything Emily. I don't have any answers." He said running his fingers through her soft hair.

"I'm not looking for any." She said, intertwining her fingers with his. Kip wound his free arm around her shoulders being careful not to hurt her. Emily bent her head and placed it on his shoulder.

Kip and Emily sat quietly, holding each other. His lips pressed against her hair. Emily knew she was in love with him and knew that pushing Kip would only push him away. It would take time for him to trust anyone with that part of his heart. She knew that and also knew that what ever happened it would be worth the wait.

****

Bernadette felt the fog that filled her head lifting and slowly the room around her came into focus. White walls with soft pine furniture. Big windows covered the far wall and a TV hung from the ceiling in the corner. The room smelled too clean. A hospital.

"Mom?" Her voice sounded foreign rolling around in her head. The figure on the couch snapped upright, head turning.

"Bernadette? Oh, Baby!" Her mother rushed across the room and fell onto the side of the bed, half kneeling, and half lying next to Bernadette. Her face was tired; wrinkles Bernadette didn't remember creased her perfect skin. She was smiling, crying and kissing her daughter.

"Mom." Bernadette wanted to lift her arms and return the hug, but she still felt heavy and awkward in her own skin.

"It's alright, everything is going to be alright."

"Where…"

"The Billings Clinic. We were so worried!" She was being hugged again. Bernadette wished the pounding in her head would stop long enough for her to enjoy being safe, warm and loved.

"How?" She forced the word out between dry lips.

"One of the men that terrorized Emily folded as soon as they started to integrate him. It took a little time before he gave up the location of the warehouse." Her mother kissed her on the forehead. "That's all behind us now. I'm just so happy to see you awake."

"Emily?" She gasped as memories flooded over her. "Emily!" Fear forced it's way into her consciousness.

"She's fine. She's here." Bernadette relaxed a bit.

"What, what happened?" The question was answered by a familiar voice.

166

"Doug, he saved us all." Kip moved from the doorway to stand near the bed, a smile playing at the edges of his lips. "Good to see you awake." Bernadette noticed his black and blue face, cuts, and to her, that needed no explanation.

"How?"

"Doug must have known that there was a chance the plan wouldn't work. He left his computer in the car you stole from Shell before you ditched it in Greybull. He turned it on, left it running…the car was found by the local police along with all the information on the flash drive."

"It was only a matter of hours from then that the news was out and everyone was on the move. The FBI had suspicions for a while about the warehouses outside of Billings, but with no solid leads." Kip was still explaining when the door opened and Emily walked into the room, her right arm in a sling.

"Oh Bernadette!" She ran to her friend. A nurse and doctor followed her into the room.

"I'm sorry, I'm going to have to ask you to leave for a moment. We need to run a few tests on Miss Brummond. If everything checks out alright then you'll be more than welcome to visit with her." The Doctor was waving Kip and Emily back out the door. He then turned back to Bernadette and smiled. "Good to see you awake."

****

Emily sat on the edge of the hospital bed smiling at Bernadette as she spooned small amounts of Jell-o into her mouth.

"You have to stop looking at me like that, you know." Bernadette said and took a sip of water.

"Sorry, I am just so happy to see you awake!" She stopped smiling. "You really had me scared you know?" Bernadette stopped eating and looked at Emily. Both girls seemed to understand what the other was unable to say.

"I still have a lot of questions." Bernadette cleared her throat.

"Shoot. I'll see if I can answer them." Emily made herself more comfortable.

"Just start from the beginning and fill me in on all the things I don't know."

"Okay. Well, I already told you about what happened to Kip and I after we left you in the cabin."

"I still can't believe that it was Professor Stevens and his group were the ones that saved both of you!"

"Yes, the irony is not lost on me." Emily and Bernadette both smiled. "Well, after the FBI got wind of us, the Lovell Hospital was pretty much over run. We were flown by helicopter to Billings and questioned. That's when we learned that you had not been found yet and about what Doug had done with the computer." Emily's voice grew soft as she talked about Doug. She could see Bernadette visibly flinch.

"If he hadn't left it on purpose, hoping it would be found, none of us would have come out of this alive. The copy on his laptop was the only one left. Once the police got their hands on it, well, it was "leaked" to the press. The FBI raided the warehouse and found you, along with about twenty other women. I use the word "women" loosely, because from what I know, most of them were teenagers."

"Do you know what happened to them? The girls." Bernadette asked, eager to know their fate.

"I was told that they are being treated for malnutrition, dehydration and I am sure post-traumatic stress. The agent that talked to Kip and I earlier said that they are working with the help of translators to contact their governments and get them home. The group

168

is pretty diverse. Some were told they would be going to school in America, or working and able to help support their families. A few were even sold by family members…" Emily shook her head. "I can't imagine… some have asked for asylum in the U.S. I guess the thought of going back to a family that sold you into slavery for money doesn't appeal to them."

"Why Wyoming and Montana? It seems like such an unlikely place." Bernadette asked.

"From what I gathered that's just why they liked this area to move the girls through. There aren't a lot of people to ask questions." Bernadette nodded and Emily continued.

"The information that Doug was able to compile from the flash drive gave the FBI a pretty detailed list of people involved and it looks like the chain of command is crumbling. There have been six other raids in four states so far." Emily smiled. "Last night, the President gave a press conference, publicly denouncing the practice of human trafficking in the United States and promising the American public that those involved would be punished to the full extent of the law."

"Wow." Was all Bernadette could croak out.

"I know! I couldn't believe it. We did that." Emily squeezed Bernadette's hand. "Doug did that."

"I can't believe it's really over." Bernadette seemed very far away as she absent mindedly reached up to touch her hair, finding it gone. Emily reached over and took her friends hand away from her shaven head. Bernadette smiled sadly and looked back at Emily. "What else?"

"Nothing really. Almost everyone involved has been arrested or fled the country. The man in the suit and a few others are the only loose ends."

"What about… us?" Bernadette asked, Emily could hear the strain in her voice.

"The FBI is keeping all of us in the hospital for a few more days. Now that you are feeling better, I'm sure you will be accosted with questions. Then, it's courtrooms for us for a while. But I think after that, well, it's back to normal life, I guess. Although, I don't think anything will be normal."

"True." Bernadette said. "What do you think Harold Pinchly was doing for all those weeks he was missing?"

"No one knows for sure, maybe leaving a false trail, maybe trying to find anyone that would help him? I don't think we'll ever know for sure." Emily shrugged a little.

"What… what are they doing…. I mean…. What about Doug?" Bernadete asked biting her lower lip. Emily could tell it was hard for Bernadette to say his name. Her voice was strained with emotion.

"I talked to his parents yesterday. They want to wait until you are released to hold his funeral." Emily's voice was nothing more than a whisper. Bernadette only nodded, her bottom lip trembling.

"I'm so sorry. I know it's not enough and I wish I could take back getting either of you involved in this mess! Oh Bernadette! Doug of all people, it shouldn't have been Doug." Emily was crying now. Tears for her friend, for the love lost, and for a life ended too soon.

Bernadette had started to sob along with Emily and the two held each other and cried. Neither said anything more. Nothing could be said. No matter the words, it would never change what had happened. Emily knew that something deep inside had been killed in Bernadette, along with Doug. It would scar her more than any of the other experiences she had endured. She felt helpless to console Bernadette. There was no way to purge the pain both of them had been feeling.

Emily stayed with Bernadette until she fell asleep. Peace finally falling over her friend's features in her dreamless state. Kip had come into the room, standing next to Emily, taking her hand in his. She felt a sense of calm falling over the room.

Emily wondered if what Bernadette said earlier about their ordeal being over could be true. She wondered if it would ever really be over for any of them. How does a person move on from an experience like theirs? There were no answers, but the absence of light was lifting, the darkness fading and at that moment she knew that whatever happened, they would weather it together.

EPILOGUE

THE END OF DAY

The sun was high in the sky; it was a warm, clear day. It was all wrong for the large crowd of people standing in a semi- circle around a freshly dug grave. Rainer sat in a well air-conditioned car, relaxing on his leather seat, cigar in hand. He had been watching the funeral procession from the time they left the church in the middle of town near the College, and drove as one of them out to the Powell cemetery.

He rolled down the window and let a long stream of smoke circle it's way out into the open air. The crowd was starting to disperse and cars pulled away leaving a few stragglers behind.

Rainer focused his gaze on three dark figures all clothed in black. The taller woman was leaning on the arm of the man standing next to her, one arm in a sling. The tall man had a hand placed on the middle of her back in a protective way. Next to her was a shorter and slightly rounder women, a black hat covered her head. He knew that it was meant to cover up her patchy hair growing back. They stood, heads bent, over the grave as the dark casket was lowered into the gaping hole, slowly swallowing it up.

Rainer felt the muscles in his body harden and flex. He was using all his restraint to stay put. He was a man of his word and the job wasn't done. A smile crossed his face and he relaxed, taking another long drag off his cigar. Now it wasn't just a job, now it was personal.

Rainer would end this. He would take care of the loose ends in his own way and in his own time. Now, *he* was pulling the strings, yet he knew he had to bide his time. Rainer was many things, but his best attribute was patience.

The End

Acknowledgments

I have been blessed with a wonderful support system and cheerleaders on my writing. Frist and foremost, my amazing husband Travis Brown who has always been supportive and encouraging even when writing took long hours and sleepless nights.

My mother and father, Lyman & Beth Sibbett, who instilled a deep love of the written word in me as a small child and have always been my frist editors, I would have never been able to realize the dream of writing a book without their help and love.

I'd also like to say "thank you" to those people that inspire my work, act as editors and sounding boards, inspired characters & book covers, story lines, and have been large part of the process in countless ways! Travis Brown, Celecia Gallagher, David & Anna Sibbett, Lori Ann Sibbett, Elena Hooper, MaKenzie, Cassie & Eliza Beck, Erica Brown, Genielle Brown, & Bobbie Brown. You have all been instrumental in my process.

About the Author

As a young child B.E. Brown found a love of writing early and began creating worlds on paper as young as 6 years old. It has continued to be a driving force throughout her life. Working on movie scripts along side her husband, writing skits, plays, short stories, and novels. Brown lives with her husband and two children in Wyoming.

Look for her other book "The Love Letters" in paperback & Kindle edition on

Amazon.com

Follow on Twitter B.E. Brown @BEBROWN3 for news on more projects,

and be looking for her newest title "Lady of Leighton Manor" coming out soon.

Made in the USA
Charleston, SC
25 November 2014